A NATALIE FUENTES MYSTERY

strange times
at Western High

EMILY POHL-WEARY

annick press
toronto + new york + vancouver

Text © 2006 Emily Pohl-Weary
Illustrations © 2006 Rose Cowles

Annick Press Ltd.

We acknowledge the support of the Canada Council for the Arts, the Ontario Arts
Council, and the Government of Canada through the Book Publishing Industry
Development Program (BPIDP) for our publishing activities.

Edited by Pam Robertson
Copy-edited and proofread by Elizabeth McLean
Cover and interior design by Irvin Cheung and Amy Lau/iCheung Design
Cover illustration by Rose Cowles
Additional image credits: drop caps on pp. 1, 15, 31, 50, 63, 80, 96, 113, 127, 146, 160,
174, 189, 202, photos on pp. 50, 99, 178, illustrations on pp. 190-191, 213, 215, and
hand lettering on pp. 37, 41, 44, 49, 90, 111, 165, 219 © Amy Lau; photos on pp. 5 and
21 © Walter Weary; photos on pp. 16, 125 © Emily Pohl-Weary; 31 © istockphoto.com;
113 © istockphoto.com/Aaron Karp; 121 © istockphoto.com/Jeff Parker; 133 © Irvin
Cheung; 183 © istockphoto.com/Pauline Vos.

Cataloguing in Publication
Pohl-Weary, Emily
Strange times at Western High/by Emily Pohl-Weary.

(A Natalie Fuentes mystery) ISBN-13: 978-1-55451-040-5 (bound) ISBN-10: 1-55451-040-
6 (bound) ISBN-13: 978-1-55451-039-9 (pbk.) ISBN-10: 1-55451-039-2 (pbk.)

I. Title. II. Series: Pohl-Weary, Emily. Natalie Fuentes mystery.
PS8631.O35S87 2006   jC813'.6   C2006-901221-0

Printed and bound in Canada

Published in the U.S.A. by	**Distributed in Canada by**	**Distributed in the U.S.A. by**
Annick Press (U.S.) Ltd.	Firefly Books Ltd.	Firefly Books (U.S.) Inc.
	66 Leek Crescent	P.O. Box 1338
	Richmond Hill, ON	Ellicott Station
	L4B 1H1	Buffalo, NY 14205

Visit our website at **www.annickpress.com**

For Beetle, Nelly and Jess,
with much love.

Chapter one

t ten minutes to nine on Natalie Fuentes's first day at Western High, the sprawling brick building with mismatched additions on either end resembled nothing more than an ant colony. Her fellow students—the ants—filed endlessly through several sets of doors. There were big ones and smaller ones, determined or anxious, some carrying huge backpacks, while others carried nothing.

Four boys wearing throwback basketball jerseys sized up everyone from their position on the front steps. A group of girls with newly cut hair and tight shirts bounced down the sidewalk, chattering happily. Two girls with glasses and overly baggy clothing passed by with their heads down.

These kids would be part of her life for the foreseeable future, Natalie realized, swallowing the dry lump in her throat. She should be used to this by now, having spent most of her sixteen years shipping out with her journalist parents, off to cover another news story in some remote part of the world... but it felt like fitting in got harder each time.

She leaned back in the banana seat of her baby blue dragster. Twisting the bicycle's handlebars sharply to the left, she rode around the school's perimeter for the second time,

squinting in the bright sunlight as she searched for a safe place to lock up.

Preoccupied, she almost missed a dark nook filled with a dozen bikes. They were locked to a collection of enormous, brightly painted steel fruit. The three walls of the cranny were covered in graffiti murals, showing students studying various subjects. Pencils, rulers, chalkboards and textbooks swirled in the air above the figures' heads.

Three girls with slightly different shades of straight blonde hair stood nearby, sharing a cigarette. They turned in unison to watch as Natalie pulled up and jumped off her bike.

Natalie smiled. They stared back, poker-faced. The one in the middle blinked. Her eyebrows raised as she took in the old, souped-up bike. Her expression mutated into a sneer as her eyes bounced down from Natalie's dark brown hair with fiery red streaks to the three piercings in her left ear, to the blue T-shirt with stencilled silver letters that said "Not Yer Princess." By the time her eyes rested on Natalie's jean miniskirt and fish-nets that ended in black boots, the girl looked like she might puke. The other two were busy assessing the middle one's expressions and rearranging their own faces accordingly.

Natalie decided the best thing was to ignore them. She found an unoccupied space next to a stripped bicycle frame that was locked to a bunch of grapes. The neon purple matched her bike better than the empty pineapple nearby. Unclipping her kryptonite lock, she took a few deep breaths. The T-shirt she was wearing had been her favorite when she picked it out last night. She'd bought it a week earlier at a zine fair in Brooklyn. All of a sudden, she hated it.

While she was fiddling with the lock, she surreptitiously examined the blondes. All three of them were wearing ruffled miniskirts in pastel shades and matching lip gloss. Their skin colors ranged from pinkish to ivory, making her deeply tanned Jewish and Argentine caramel skin seem that much darker. They all had blue eyes, but Natalie thought at least one of them was wearing colored contacts.

The leader noticed Natalie looking over. She scrunched up her face like a bulldog and spat: "What are you staring at?"

Natalie looked away, scowling.

"Hey! Don't ignore me," grated the girl. "I asked you a question."

"Not much," said Natalie.

The girls tittered and huddled together. The one who'd spoken whispered something to the other two, who sneered and glanced over at Natalie.

Great, she thought. She'd managed to make enemies before first period. Not wanting to walk past them again, she hesitated by her bike, pretending to search for something important in her bag. No matter where her parents dragged her, it was the same old game at every school: make the new kid suffer. Her skin really should have grown thicker by now.

This day was definitely shaping up badly. She'd woken up as planned to her alarm CD player blaring her current musical obsession, the Broken Social Scene, but things rapidly went downhill from there. She'd crawled into the shower only to discover her favorite gel was still in an unopened box in her bedroom, and was forced to settle for her dad's sticky pot of pomade.

She'd done her best with her hair. Needless to say, it was a huge mess that lay flat on top of her head and poked out at weird angles near her shoulders. She'd been going for the layered flip the hairstylist had attained at the salon last week, but ended up with something more like the Scarecrow in *The Wizard of Oz*—if he'd had greasy brown and red hair. A loser hairdo was the last thing she would have wished for today.

Just then, a boy wearing the standard jock uniform—shapeless jeans, a cotton T-shirt saying Western Mustangs Senior Football and brand-new cross-trainers—sped up to a bike stand. He leaped off his battered mountain bike, frantically threw it against the empty pineapple and locked it in one fluid motion. He glanced at Natalie but didn't smile, just widened his eyes. Then he was off running. On his way past, he called out a greeting to the blondes, who unenthusiastically quirked up their mouths in response, and promptly started to diss him behind his back. At least he'd momentarily distracted them from Natalie.

She could have kissed someone when she noticed a metal service door propped open with a piece of wood. Instead of passing the girls to go in through the front entrance, maybe she could just duck inside the school that way. Save herself a huge headache. Plus, she was a firm believer that the less traveled route was always more interesting. Ignoring the voice in her head warning that her instincts had been known to get her into a load of trouble in the past, she slipped through the door before the girls could turn back to her.

Natalie found herself in a long hallway with crates piled against both walls. On her right was the back entrance to the cafe-

teria, judging by the pungent smell of food being prepared. On the left was a door with a sign on it: Isaac Kaufman, Chief Caretaker.

On the wall nearby was an antique print of Jerusalem, hanging from leather strips attached to a thin wood pole. Must have been the caretaker's. Natalie liked the personal touch. She reached into her shoulder bag and pulled out her constant companion: her digital camera. The art and the sign together might make a nice graphic for her zine, *My Very Secret Life*.

Clicking a few shots, she noticed the caretaker's door was held ajar with a mop. She could hear men's voices behind it. They seemed to be arguing.

Not wanting to get in trouble, she quietly tiptoed toward the unmarked door at the far end of the hall. A few steps past the caretaker's room, she heard swearing. A man's voice ground out something along the lines of "keep your mouth shut." It sounded threatening.

She froze. Torn between checking out the situation and hurrying along to her appointment with the school principal, she strained to hear what was going on. A muffled cry, a loud crash and the sound of breaking glass clinched her decision. She flung open the door and ran out onto a metal platform above the sunken floor of the caretaker's office.

"Everything all right?" she called out. She heard the sharp clatter of footsteps down below, in a part of the room she couldn't see, and then everything went silent. In front of her, the walls were lined to the ceiling with fastidiously organized metal shelves holding all the spare parts that kept the school running smoothly: nails, bolts, light bulbs, paint cans, tools and cleaning supplies.

Gripping the railing, she descended the ladder-like industrial staircase. When she was about halfway down, she turned to peer at the back half of the room through the steps, trying to locate the person whose footsteps she'd heard.

What a mess! A tangle of papers belched out of a filing cabinet and the contents of several desk drawers spewed across the floor. The desk itself was completely bare, except for an old laser printer sitting at one end. The telephone that used to be on top of it lay nearby, ripped from the wall. A computer monitor was upside down on the floor, broken glass scattered around it. The rest of the machine lay on its side, cables slithering out of its back.

Natalie took shallow, nervous breaths as she scanned the room. She couldn't see any exits other than the one back up the industrial staircase she was standing on. Whoever caused this mess was still in here.

She got to the bottom, passed two tall gray metal cupboards and slowly rounded the desk. When she glanced down, she screamed and stumbled backward. A thin white-haired man wearing a pair of green overalls was curled up on the floor and his hair was matted with blood.

She bent down to feel for his pulse but was too freaked out to locate it. Her hands were shaking. She should call for help, she realized. She picked up the office phone, but since its cord was pulled out there was no dial tone. Duh. She put it back down and rooted around in the bottom of her bag to find the cell phone her father had given her for emergencies. She kept forgetting she was carrying it.

She glanced at the phone's display and her heart sank.

It didn't work down here. Some help it was! While she hesitated with the phone in her hand, wondering what to do, the cupboard doors flew open with a bang. A wiry body hurtled toward her. She caught a glimpse of a bulky hooded sweatshirt and a ski mask hiding the person's face from view. Then she was body-checked so hard she lurched backward and dropped the phone.

Instinctively, she grabbed a handful of sweatshirt to steady herself. A vicious twist of her wrist and a punch to the forearm made her let go and sent her reeling into the desk, but not before the navy blue pullover the man was wearing hiked up his arm to expose a gold and silver watch with a reddish-orange logo on it.

She fell into a corner of the desk and the air slammed out of her lungs. Some stroke of luck allowed her to catch herself on the edge or she would have toppled right onto the janitor. She twisted to get another look at the intruder racing up the stairs and out the door. All she could see were black pants and expensive running shoes. And now that he'd straightened up, she noticed he was taller than he'd seemed when he barreled into her.

Natalie pushed herself upright and looked around for her cell phone. It was lying at the base of the cupboard. She retrieved it and dropped it back into her bag. At the same time, she pulled out a long-sleeved cotton shirt, which she twisted into a thick rope and tied around the unconscious man's head. She didn't want to move his neck, but knew she should apply pressure to the wound.

Next, she inspected the desk phone, which was still on

the floor. The little prong on its jack appeared to have broken off, but it was otherwise intact. When she inserted it into the wall socket and held it there, she got a dial tone. She called emergency response and gave the operator as much information as possible about the man's injuries and his precise location. The operator said an ambulance would be there in five minutes. Natalie hung up and replaced the phone on the desk.

She made her way up the stairs and into the hallway, where she discovered that the unmarked door at the end of the hall did indeed exit into the school's first floor. She paused to ask a student where the principal's office was, and then ran off in that direction.

Right outside the office door stood a large-boned woman wearing a fitted brown leather outfit that set off her light brown skin and holding a clipboard at chest level, who could only be Principal Jefferson. She was explaining to a dozen new students how to read their timetables. They all looked as apprehensive as Natalie'd been feeling moments ago. She was actually supposed to be one of them, attending her first orientation session.

"Ms. Jefferson?" asked Natalie urgently.

The principal spun around, lips compressed. "Natalie Fuentes? We've been waiting for you." She jammed a sheaf of papers into Natalie's hands without waiting for an explanation. "I don't know what standards your last school set for its students, but I will not tolerate tardiness at Western High."

"I'm sorry. I... I was held up in the basement."

"The basement is off-limits to students."

"Um. Isaac Kaufman, the caretaker, was attacked."

The other students jolted awake. The principal let the clipboard fall to her side. "Oh no! Not again."

"It's happened before?" asked Natalie.

Jefferson didn't respond. She just jerked her head a couple of times and dashed into the office, barking at a man sitting in a room marked Vice-Principal that there'd been an emergency and he should finish up the orientation. She rushed back out clutching a blank incident report in one hand. With the other, she clasped Natalie's forearm firmly. Natalie winced and pulled loose as they marched down the hall. The intruder must have hit her pretty hard. A big purple bruise was spreading across her arm. Jefferson didn't seem to notice.

"I was outside the door when I heard yelling and a crash," said Natalie, annoyed she wasn't being given any information after what she'd just gone through. "What's going on? This isn't the first time he's been attacked?"

Again, Jefferson didn't answer Natalie's questions, at least not directly. "Your last principal said your family moves around a lot—something about journalist parents. Well, listen up, young lady, nosiness is not rewarded here at Western. Understand? Leave the dangerous situations to me."

"Fine," said Natalie, rolling her eyes as she hurried to keep up.

Principal Jefferson pulled a set of master keys out of her pocket and opened the door to the caretaker's hallway, which must have locked behind Natalie. They found a team of people already in the room. Two police officers were just starting to put up yellow crime scene tape around the messy office, and paramedics were preparing to move the unconscious man to a stretcher.

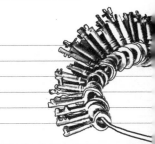

Another cop, holding a little spiral notepad, turned as they entered and spoke to Natalie. "Are you the girl who called emergency response?"

"Yes."

"You saw the accident?" asked the same cop.

Natalie nodded, then shook her head in confusion. "No. Well, I heard it. I was walking past the door when I heard fighting and a big crash. Mr. Kaufman—at least I assume it's him— cried out."

Jefferson snorted. "I *do* have a snoop on my hands."

"Please continue, miss," said the cop, frowning, pen poised above his notepad.

"I heard footsteps," said Natalie, "then I saw him lying there, surrounded by all this mess. A man wearing a ski mask was hiding in that cupboard, but I didn't know at the time. I was trying to call an ambulance when he burst out and banged into me, knocked me over." She held up her arm to demonstrate the bruise.

Jefferson started to say something, but the police officer spoke first: "Young lady, you did the right thing. Your phone call may very well have saved this man's life." He glanced over at Isaac Kaufman, who was being strapped onto the stretcher by the paramedics.

The cop was a brick wall of a man, with a bulbous pink nose, and hair so short he almost looked bald. He asked Natalie to follow him to the far side of the room so he could speak with her in private. By leading her away, he effectively forced his partner to deal with Principal Jefferson, who was now sputtering about emergency procedures.

"I'm Detective Carl Lewis," he said, pumping Natalie's hand with his much larger one.

"Natalie Fuentes," she said.

She answered his slew of questions in a daze, telling him everything that happened, minute details about what the attacker looked like, and why she'd been in this part of the school, while she watched Principal Jefferson hover over the paramedics. They secured the old man's head and carted the stretcher up the stairs and off to the waiting ambulance. Jefferson trailed along behind, demanding to know what hospital they were taking him to.

"Do you remember anything else about the man?" Lewis was asking.

Natalie's head felt foggy. She had to struggle to think about specifics. "He was wearing a watch under the sweatshirt."

"Did you see his skin color?"

She shook her head. "He had black gloves."

"Any other identifying features? His eyes or face?"

"No. The mask and hood covered everything. It all happened so fast…"

"Well, then, I suppose I'm finished here," said Lewis, finally flipping his notepad closed. "Thanks for your time, Natalie. Here's my card. If you think of anything else, give me a call. A detective will be here very soon to take your fingerprints. We need to be able to compare them to any others we find at the crime scene."

She expected him to attend to other work, but instead he just leaned back against a nearby wall and surveyed the scene.

The door above them screeched open, and to Natalie's surprise, a boy her age entered. He had messy black hair and wore baggy navy cords and dark green high-top sneakers. A faded brown camp T-shirt hung off his thin frame. Large silver headphones covered his ears.

He took in the crowd of people. A look of shock registered on his face, then he tore off the headphones and rushed down the stairs. "What's going on?"

Natalie was closest to him. She forced herself to form coherent words. "I was in the hall. Heard a crash, and... then a yell... I... um..."

"You *what*?"

Detective Lewis stepped forward. "This is a crime scene. You shouldn't be in here."

The boy pushed wire-framed glasses up the bridge of his nose. "What do you mean, I shouldn't be here? This is my father's office! Where is he?" His eyes darted around, assessing the mess.

"I'm sorry, son, but your father's been injured. He was taken to the hospital."

The boy blanched. "What happened? Is he OK?"

"The paramedics are caring for him, thanks to this young lady," added Lewis.

The boy spun toward Natalie. "You saw what happened?"

Natalie gulped and shook her head. "No. I heard it. He was attacked. And I saw the guy who did it, but he was wearing a ski mask."

"Who are you? Why don't I know you?" he demanded impatiently.

"I'm Natalie Fuentes. I just transferred here."

"Oh." He scrubbed his eyes with the back of his hand. He bore a marked resemblance to the man on the ground, she noticed. His face was unusual: mouth a little wide, skin pale even though the summer was just ending. Definitely not a jock.

Principal Jefferson pushed open the door and came back into the room, alone. Her face was grim, deep lines creasing her forehead. She ran a hand through her short curly hair when she saw the boy standing there. "Jacob, there you are. I was just about to call you out of class. The paramedics say your father will be fine. He's been taken to Toronto General. If you come with me, I'll drive you over to the hospital."

Lewis cleared his throat. "We'll want to ask him some questions first."

"For god's sake, ask them later! His father's just been attacked."

"Oh... of course. Well, how about I follow you two over to the hospital and speak to the boy there?"

Jacob shrugged numbly. Jefferson shook her head in annoyance, but didn't argue. She steered Jacob up the stairs and out of the room. Lewis strode off after them.

A few minutes later, two detectives came in. One of them opened a fingerprint kit and started to dust the office area for prints, using a soft brush that looked as if it should be part of a makeup kit and some wide cellophane tape. The other one got set up and came over, pressed each of Natalie's fingers into an inky pad, and placed them one at a time on a piece of paper with boxes for all ten digits. When he was done, he asked her all of the same questions the previous officer had.

Natalie was left feeling like there were cotton balls in her brain. Disoriented, she trudged up the stairs and into the school, reading her timetable. It was already eleven—halfway through her last morning class.

Instead of finding her way to geography, or heading home like she really wanted to do, she went outside and wandered around the school grounds until she found a quiet courtyard. She slumped down next to a young maple tree and pulled out the diary she filled with ephemera to be used as inspiration for future issues of *My Very Secret Life*. On the cover were a cat and dog dressed as pirates. Below them, it said: "Let's hook up."

The image usually made her smile. Today she just heaved a sigh, then turned to a clean page, licked each of her inky fingers, and pressed them down. After circling and labeling each print, she started to write down a few notes about the morning. Things she wanted to remember. Like how it felt to get hit that way, and what the intruder had been wearing.

All too soon, the double doors nearby opened and the first students wandered out to enjoy their lunch break: a clump of Goths, dressed entirely in black, eyes heavily lined with kohl. They were making fun of the girls who came out after them, dressed primly in floral prints and carrying huge stacks of books. Then came the three girls Natalie'd encountered that morning. The head girl saw her sitting there alone, and shot her a glare.

Excellent. By lunchtime on her first day, Natalie'd managed to witness a brutal attack, get on the principal's bad side, *and* make an enemy of the queen of the ant hill. It was a record, even for her.

chapter two

ath was Natalie's first class after lunch. The teacher, Mr. Wojcik, turned out to be an imposing man with a handlebar mustache. He didn't get much teaching done, just passed out textbooks, went over a class outline and told a few lame jokes. He also seemed to be speaking directly to four guys sitting at the back of the room, which was fortunate, because all Natalie could think about was that little man, unconscious on the stretcher, and his strange, shell-shocked son.

At one point, she pulled herself out of her thoughts long enough to turn in her seat and get a good look at the boys behind her. One of them smirked at her and mouthed the words: "Nice hair." His buddy guffawed.

Natalie quickly faced forward again, cheeks burning. A tiny girl with glasses sitting nearby stopped chewing her Hello Kitty pen long enough to hiss: "Ignore Mark and Jamie. Wojcik's the football coach. Jocks love this class."

"Perfect," Natalie whispered back, sarcastically. Math wasn't her favorite subject. And as for football, well, she could never figure out why otherwise sane boys would choose to put on stinky uniforms and get bashed around in the mud for three hours.

Her last period of the day was English, and for that she

was better able to focus. She liked the quiet little Mr. Wallace for three reasons: his reading list for the term didn't include a single Shakespeare play, he didn't make bad jokes and he didn't seem to favor the jocks.

When school ended, Natalie located her locker near the gymnasium on the second floor, tossed her textbooks inside and headed out to retrieve her bike. Entering the cranny, she was relieved to see the blonde girls weren't around. Instead, a group of boys wearing baggy jeans had taken over the space. Two of them held spray cans, had bandanas tied over their faces, and were getting instructions from a third about how to touch up the wall mural in places where the paint was fading or peeling off.

She approached the bike stands hesitantly. The guys who'd been working on the mural turned and slouched into tough-guy poses. The one who'd been giving them orders muttered something under his breath, then whistled loudly— the universal mating call. He lifted dark sunglasses onto his slicked-back hair and crooned: "*Ai, chica*, I must be asleep to dream of such beauty."

His accent sounded Chilean. Natalie gave him a frosty glare and turned her back. She swallowed a correspondingly cheesy putdown, figuring she'd already made enough enemies for one day. An unwanted compliment or two was no biggie after spending a month in Buenos Aires this summer with her father, following her parents' separation. *Piropo*, what the Argentines called "street poetry," was the country's second-most popular sport. Soccer was first, of course.

Besides, she had more important things to think about.

Like why hadn't Principal Jefferson been in touch since the accident? Was Isaac Kaufman all right? Had Natalie missed anything important during the morning's orientation?

Mind racing, she rode through sleepy residential streets shaded by grand old maple trees, evergreens and decorative gardens, turned down a street lined with mid-sized brownstones—all variations on a single theme—and swung into a short driveway. Her new home was bland turn-of-the-century-style brick, three slim stories high, with dark green trim and a huge front porch that stretched from one side to the other.

It looked sturdy enough, she decided. It would do. She and her father had only moved in three days ago, so it still felt vaguely like someone else's house that they were camping out in.

After locking up her bike on the porch, she opened the front door and entered the small coatroom that fed directly into an open-concept living/dining room. Her father had obviously spent the entire day setting things up. The furniture was artfully arranged, floor-to-ceiling wall shelves were neatly filled with books, and the stereo was playing his favorite Mercedes Sosa album.

Their cordless phone was flashing: a new message. She picked it up and listened to an urgent request from Principal Jefferson, asking for Natalie's father to call her immediately. Natalie jotted down the number and deleted the message. When Mercedes started belting out the song "Como Pajaros en el Aire," she switched off the music and headed through to the kitchen.

Jorge Fuentes, her dad, sat at an island in the middle of the room, sipping from a steaming mug of sweet black tea. The

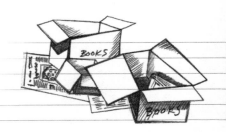

sleeves of his casual button-down shirt were rolled up, and he was reading the *Toronto Star*. The paper had just hired him full-time, which was the reason they were both living in this new city.

He looked up as she approached and his warm brown eyes caught hers. Her face must have shown how she was feeling, because he said her nickname softly, like a question: "Nati?"

She greeted him the Argentine way, with air kisses next to both cheeks. "Sorry. That song about how Mercedes's mother's hands are like little birds flying through the air reminds me too much of mom."

He did his signature shrug — half-nod, half-shoulder scrunch. "Would you prefer Horacio Guarany?"

"Um, no tango."

"It's not tango, *mihija*. It's *canciones folklóricas*."

"Folk songs, whatever. That music's depressing me right now," she grumbled.

Somehow he'd managed to scrounge together his favorite afternoon snack: crusty white bread, jam and hard cheese. Her stomach growled. She'd been too worked up to eat anything at lunchtime. She searched through cupboards until she found where he'd unpacked the mugs, slid onto a stool and helped herself to some tea. Taking small, rapid sips, she willed the caffeine to enter her bloodstream.

"You're cheery today," he quipped. "How was your first day at school?"

"Mmph."

"I'll take that to mean 'not good.'"

She indicated he was on to something with a tilt of her

head, and took a larger gulp of tea. The hot liquid scalded her mouth, brought tears to her eyes.

"The bread is delicious," he prodded. "I went out for a jog this afternoon and discovered a little bakery just two blocks away."

Natalie grimaced at the thought of jogging, then ripped off a hunk of crusty baguette and slathered it with jam. After stuffing it in her mouth, she described her day at school, beginning with her schedule and teachers, working her way up to missing her morning classes because she'd witnessed the attack.

"Were you hurt?" he asked.

"Nah."

"Then let me get this straight," he said incredulously. "You saw a janitor beaten unconscious and just decided to stay at school for the rest of the day, as if nothing had happened?"

"Well, I didn't think... Kind of."

"Tell me again," he said, much too slowly, "how you managed to be outside this man's office at the exact moment when he was being attacked."

"Shortcut."

Her father raised an eyebrow. "Oh, I see. One of your infamous shortcuts."

"Some really mean girls were standing between me and all of the school's main entrances."

"What I don't understand is why nobody called to tell me about this."

She slumped down into her chair. "Actually, someone did. My principal. I just listened to a message from her, asking you to call her." She handed over the message.

He looked at her with concern. "I didn't hear the phone ring."

"Your music was on pretty loud."

He stood up and strode into the living room, came back dialing the phone. Obviously it clicked through to the office's answering service, because he left a message for Jefferson to call him at his new office in the morning. He threw the phone onto the pile of newspapers and sat back down. "At least you're okay."

"Right. Except for one little bruise."

"How little?" he asked sharply.

She pushed up her sleeve to show him her forearm.

He let out a low whistle. "That's no little bruise! You should put ice on it..."

"Too late for that." She shoved the sleeve back down. "Any swelling has already happened. Besides, it barely hurts anymore."

He looked skeptical. "Nati, promise you'll be more careful from now on."

"I promise."

He didn't look convinced.

Wanting to give him time to cool off, Natalie picked up the arts section of the paper and read an article about a local artist who'd created a series of digitally "beautified" CN Towers. When they'd been driving into town on the expressway, her father had pointed out the tower, the world's tallest, a penlike structure that poked the skyline from Toronto's downtown core. In the image accompanying the story, the artist had turned the tower's red, yellow and green elevators, which were visible from the outside, into ketchup, mustard and relish bottles. The circular bulge two-thirds of the way up—a restaurant and viewing station—was now a giant burger. She ripped out the picture for her scrapbook.

When she glanced over at her father again, he didn't look quite as upset as he had before. He was skimming the sports section.

"So. Any plans for tonight?" she asked casually.

"Take a guess."

"Unpacking and more unpacking?"

"The precocious girl whose hair clashes with her T-shirt wins a prize!"

This sounded so funny coming from her father, like Bob Barker from *The Price is Right* with a thick Argentine accent, that she laughed out loud. "Come on, I'm already feeling sensitive about this shirt. Those blonde girls hated it."

"Who's teasing?" he asked dryly, holding up the paper in front of his face.

She curled down a corner and peered at him. There was no hint of sarcasm on his face. In fact, he was trying his best to look innocent. "Well, I was wondering if you could drive me to the hospital to visit Isaac Kaufman."

He frowned. "Not on your life. I know you want to make sure he's all right, but you really shouldn't be getting involved in this."

"I'm already involved! I found the man lying there on the floor. I wrapped his head to slow the bleeding. I called the police." She held up her hands to show him her black fingertips. "They questioned me for *hours*."

He peered intently at her hands. "Why do you have to go down there? Why not just call?"

"Hospitals don't give out information over the phone. It's like a *law* or something."

"So I suppose you wouldn't listen to me if I forbid you from going."

He knew her so well.

Jorge sighed. "Which hospital is he at?"

"Toronto General."

"Okay, I'll drive you there and pick you up, then. I can make a trip over to my new office and drop off some things while you're inside. Shouldn't take me more than an hour."

Natalie shoved a last bite of bread into her mouth. "Thanks, Dad!"

"Wait! I have two conditions…"

"Anything."

"One, you be very careful. You don't know this man or why he was attacked. And, two, this morning, our next-door neighbor Cathy Hamilton came by to welcome us to the neighborhood. She made the delicious homemade jam you're eating right now. She has two kids around your age who go to Western High and suggested you ride your bikes to school together."

She groaned. Oh, no! Not that. "Dad, don't try to make friends for me. It never goes well. Remember when you introduced me to those American sisters in Madrid? They stole my lunch for an entire week, until I got even by packing a chicken sandwich with bad meat in it."

He frowned. "Ugh. Yes, well, you're shy, Nati…"

"I'm not shy! I select my friends *very* carefully."

"This will be good for you." He lifted up the paper again. "Besides, you've already agreed."

She picked up her newspaper clipping. "Fine. Just don't expect me to like them."

"Thank you, Nati."

Belatedly feeling a pang of guilt for being difficult—her dad was the only ally she had at the moment—she paused on her way through the living room and popped the Guarany disc into the stereo. A bolero about the hard-livin' cowboy *gauchos* from Patagonia came on. Listening to the well-worn album was a small price to pay for her father's happiness. Besides, she would barely be able to hear it upstairs.

Her new bedroom was at the back of the house. She booted up her computer and put on the All Girl Summer Fun Band. She hung a poster of Kathleen Cleaver on the wall, and some cover art from the first four issues of *My Very Secret Life*. Emily the Strange went above her desk. She filled the top of her dresser with assorted photographs, including a few of her mother. The room was starting to feel a little more cozy, a little more her own. After moving so much, she'd become an expert at this: just take an empty room, add posters, a computer and a good indie band. Presto! Insta-home!

She sat down at the computer, checked her email, and chatted online with her New York friends while she Googled the Toronto General Hospital. The website listed a patient information phone number, which she called to confirm that Isaac Kaufman was still there. They told her he was in the ICU on the first floor.

Next, she popped his name into the search engine and

came up with lots of hits for that name, but none of them were Western High's caretaker. She added the qualifier of Toronto and found a mention of him on a school board employee list. There were also a couple of short articles about the first attack, dated eight months ago. He was jumped from behind on his way to the school parking lot. The police never made any arrests, but an unknown male beat him so badly he was left with a broken arm and an acute concussion. Two concussions in less than a year, she thought, grimacing. That can't be good for a person.

Curiosity piqued, she searched for Jacob Kaufman and got hundreds of direct hits. He was clearly some sort of super nerd. She waded through posts he'd made to a newsgroup during the last couple of years. Most of them were way beyond her—too technical. She moved on to 2600.com, a site called The Hacker Quarterly, where there was a brief essay he'd written. As she read, her eyes widened.

Unauthorized Computer Access
by Jacob Kaufman, Toronto

Last month, I was arrested for "Unauthorized Use Of A Computer." Three plain-clothes detectives came to my house after school, arrested me, cuffed me and took me to a holding cell. I was strip-searched (they were looking for codes, I guess???) and held in custody for six hours.

All because I was using my cousin's account to distribute my

Anarchist newsletter, *The Anarchives*. I naively thought I had freedom of speech. It turns out that freedom in cyberspace, like in the real world, must be authorized. And only an ISP's system administrator has that authority.

I was scared. My life was suddenly made public, and I was desperate to get it back. Fortunately, my dad found a good lawyer, who was dedicated to helping me out. In the end, the charges were dropped, although not until several months later, after numerous appearances in court, and I agreed to never access the service provider's network again.

This incident is indicative of the state of our so-called information highway. Do people have any rights online in the first place? What right do system administrators have to turn information over to the cops? Who are the "authorities" on the Internet—companies, system administrators, or the cops?

So, Jacob had been arrested for hacking two months after his dad was attacked the first time. Natalie pictured the smashed computer lying on the ground in his father's office. What if the intruder had deliberately targeted it?

At the bottom of the essay was a link to Jacob's personal site, where he'd apparently posted old issues of his newsletter. Clicking through, she found his personal blog and read comments from other people about Jacob's case. It seemed as if the arrest had made him into a bit of a hero. People kept calling him a "hacktivist" sacrificed to the "rule of lawlessness," to distinguish him from malicious "crackers." Whatever Jacob was, he definitely knew his way around computer networks, and that probably included his father's work terminal.

Jorge yelled up to say he was ready to head out. She quickly bookmarked Jacob's site before running downstairs. On the way to the hospital, she flipped through radio stations to avoid conversation.

When her father pulled up to the curb, she was astonished they'd arrived so quickly. Toronto was much smaller than New York. It only took ten minutes to get downtown. Her dad pressed some money into her palm with a request that she pick up dinner at the sandwich shop next door, and they made plans to meet out front in an hour. She got out of the car and headed to the information desk, told a little white lie—that she was Isaac Kaufman's daughter—and was directed to the intensive care unit.

A stern-faced nurse sitting behind a desk covered with paper guarded the automated double doors to the ICU. Natalie greeted the nurse and asked to be allowed in to see her father, alarmed at the ease with which lies were popping out of her mouth.

The nurse barely looked up, just reached over and pushed a button. "Third bed on your right."

Natalie entered the ICU and immediately spotted Jacob in a vinyl armchair with his feet resting against the edge of his dad's bed and a laptop propped up on his knees. He was playing a video game with elves and dwarves doing battle. There were no other visitors. Not that Isaac Kaufman cared—the man lay unmoving beneath the hospital linens, hooked up with tubes and wires to several machines that beeped and flashed. He looked much the same as he had when she'd found him on the floor.

"Hi, Jacob," she said.

He glanced up, bleary-eyed. "Natalie, right? How'd you get in here?"

She pulled up a chair and sat down. "Told the nurse I'm your sister."

"My sister?"

"I was afraid they wouldn't let me in otherwise. I've been really worried about your dad. Hadn't heard anything since this morning."

He didn't respond, just saved his game and slipped the laptop into the backpack at his feet. He was acting like it made total sense that some stranger would be concerned with his dad's well-being. But when his eyes bounced back up to her face, they were filled with worry.

"How's he doing?" she asked gently.

He squeezed his eyes shut for a second, probably fighting back tears. "They think he had a mild stroke. He threw up a couple times when he first woke up, because of the concussion, but seems to be doing a little better the past hour or two. Resting calmly and not as dizzy when he's awake. The doctors keep telling me he's going to be fine. So, I guess he is."

Natalie wondered why Jacob's mother wasn't here, if his parents were divorced like hers. She wanted to ask about the arrest and his dad's computer, but figured it was against hospital rules to badger immediate family members into revealing personal information while their loved ones lay nearby. Besides, Jacob was clearly exhausted. There were dark circles under his eyes. She'd been so determined to come to the hospital. Now she felt rude for intruding.

After a time, she cleared her throat, needing to break the eerie background rhythm of bleeping machines. "And you?"

"What about me?"

"How're you doing?"

"I'm not the one who got hit on the head."

"No, but you look really tired. Have you eaten anything? I forgot to eat lunch, and I..."

"I'm not hungry," he said shortly.

She paused, then tried again. "Well, I'm just asking because my dad gave me more than enough money to buy us dinner at the sandwich shop next door. We don't have much food in the house... just moved in on Friday."

He slumped further down in his chair. "I'm fine."

"It's so obvious you're not fine."

"Leave me alone."

"No way," she said. "I can't do that."

"Trust me, it's safer for everyone if you just forget about what happened this morning."

She lifted her sleeve to show him the bruise. "Look, Jacob. Whoever did this to your dad saw my face too. I'm sure he knows who I am."

Jacob's face tightened a fraction.

"I'm going to buy you dinner, Jacob. Either come with me and pick something yourself or else I'll choose and bring it back here. There's no way you thought to stop for money on your way to the hospital, even if you did somehow manage to collect your laptop."

"It was already in my bag."

"What, is it like your security blanket?" she blurted out,

and immediately regretted it. What was her problem? Most of the time, she was a fairly polite person. The stress must be getting to her.

He gave her a funny look, but to her astonishment he picked up his backpack and led the way out. They made their way to the sandwich shop, which was connected to the hospital's main lobby by an archway. It was filled with the oddest array of diners. A few harried-looking businessmen and women spotted the room. Several escaped patients, still wearing scrubs, had also wheeled their IV poles down from their hospital rooms, and sat there eating with tubes connected to their arms. Obviously, they preferred making the trek over eating another bite of rubbery hospital food.

She ordered a turkey on rye for herself and an egg salad to go for her dad. Jacob got a vegetarian sub. She polished off her enormous sandwich, then sat watching Jacob pick at his food listlessly for ten minutes. He was so depressed. She cast around for something to distract him—anything—and settled for demonstrating the fine art of photographing people without their knowledge by pretending to focus on something else and moving the camera at the last second. That made him glance around for the first time and notice their strange dinner companions. He looked surprised. She snapped a shot of him like that and leaned over to show him.

"So, what, is that camera like your security blanket?" he joked.

She smiled. "I guess. Everything that happens, no matter how bad, just becomes material for my zine."

He looked at her curiously. "You make a zine?"

Curiosity was way better than depression. By a long shot. "I'll give you some back issues, as soon as I get a chance to make more. I sold out at a zine fair in Brooklyn last weekend."

Finding out she was from New York inevitably led him to ask why she'd moved to Toronto. She kept up a steady stream of chit-chat until it was time to go meet her father out front, revealing more about her family situation than she normally would have. Only because, while he was listening, he was also eating. And, considering how much she already knew about him, it was only fair. She told him about the divorce and how she was living with her dad while her mother traipsed around the world. "Right now, she's god knows where, being an intrepid, single lady journalist."

"Wow, so you don't actually know where she is?"

"She's in France right now, but she goes wherever she's sent for a story."

He glanced in the direction of the ICU. "At least I know how to find my father. I don't know if he's safe, but I know where he is."

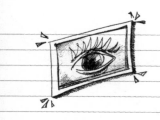

chapter three

The next morning, as Natalie was unlocking her bike, she heard singing. A girl sat on the lawn next door with her back to the house. She was doing some kind of weird leg stretch, and belting out a tune that sounded vaguely like "Stayin' Alive," the Bee Gees' song from that awful movie that was always on late-night TV. A green bicycle with a rainbow of hand-painted flowers on its frame lay prone beside her.

"Hey there," said Natalie, wheeling up.

The girl twisted around, causing her curly blonde hair to bounce away from her head. "Oh, hi! I didn't hear you come outside. You're Natalie from New York, right? My mom told me. I wanted to go to New York for a weekend this summer, but my parents think it's too dangerous. Is it dangerous?"

Natalie shrugged. "Not if you know how to stay out of trouble."

"They're totally lame," the girl pouted. "I read that the *Rocky Horror Picture Show* is going to get another run on Broadway. All new cast, including Freddie Prinze Jr. as Brad. That'd be so awesome. I'm dying to see it. Ever been to a show on Broadway?"

Natalie nodded. She refrained from adding that she hoped this piece of gossip didn't have any truth behind

it. An army of flawless Hollywood stars carrying laser guns couldn't force her to see that musical mangled by Freddie.

"I'm sorry. I forgot to introduce myself," said the girl. "I'm Ruth. My brother Matt will be out in a moment." Ruth suddenly folded forward into a painful-looking stretch. She mumbled from somewhere around her kneecap: "I've never had a neighbor who's the same age as me. You *are* the same age as me, right? Sixteen?"

Natalie nodded, then realized Ruth couldn't see her head from that angle. "Yeah, I am."

"That is so cool. And you transferred into Western High. Nobody transfers into Western these days! Out, sure, but not in."

"My dad says it's the best school in the area."

Ruth sat upright and shook out her legs. "Sure, it's a good school. But with all the weird things happening lately, students are being yanked out left and right. My parents even threatened to send me and Matt to Northern…"

"What do you mean, weird things?" interrupted Natalie.

Ruth picked up her bike. "You name it. Teachers quitting. People being attacked. Vandalism. Equipment going missing. Weird stickers and graffiti appearing on the walls. Stuff getting moved around. The principal had to cut back on all the sports programs because there's not enough money in the budget to replace the stolen stuff."

"What stuff?"

"You name it, it's gone. Baseballs, bats, helmets, hockey sticks, soccer balls, flags, nets…everything."

"Oh, well, I'm not much into sports," said Natalie, waving a hand in dismissal.

"My brother is. He's a year older than me, the junior football quarterback. The coach says that if he continues like this, he'll be voted Most Valuable Player and could even be recruited for the CFL..." She stopped abruptly and groaned. "I'm talking too much, aren't I? My brother says a talky-talky demon takes over my mouth, like in this episode of *Star Trek* where the..."

"You *are* a bit of a talker," said a boy's voice, coming from inside the Hamiltons' front door.

"Shut up, Matt!" snapped Ruth, rolling her eyes. "Why do you always have to listen in on *my* conversations? And come outside so Natalie can meet you."

A figure emerged from the house, a rangy, athletic-looking boy who bore a strong resemblance to his sister. It was strange to see a face that gentle on a boy, though. His warm grin just made it even stranger. This was the football quarterback?

"Natalie, meet my least favorite brother, Matt."

"I'm your only brother," he corrected, eyes narrowing to slits.

"Whatever. Let's go or we'll be late for school."

Matt snorted in irritation, and headed around the side of the house. He was walking an expensive-looking gold and black bicycle toward them when Ruth leaped on her bike and sped off without waiting. Feeling a little awkward, Natalie followed along more leisurely, forcing the girl to slow down. Soon enough, Matt was riding alongside them.

"So, you just moved in?" he asked Natalie, conversationally.

"On Saturday."

"Guess you don't know too many people at school, then."

"So far I've met exactly three, other than you guys. One of

them was Principal Jefferson and another was unconscious."

"What?"

"Isaac Kaufman."

"Wait a minute," said Ruth. "You're the student who saw the attack!"

"Personally, I think his son Jacob is one weird dude," said Matt, shaking his head as he turned a corner. "I heard he was arrested last year, for hacking or something."

"I read that on the Internet," said Natalie. "Apparently, it was a big misunderstanding."

"Right. Well, he sure knows a lot about computers. His laptop is practically an extension of his arms. And his dad has really bad luck. Imagine getting jumped twice in one year."

"Serious bad luck," she repeated, nodding. Quite possibly more than that too.

"I think Jacob's cute, in a geeky way," said Ruth.

Her brother laughed, a short burst. "Ruth, he's more of a surly nerd than a mysterious hacker."

"He's always been sweet to me," defended Ruth.

"So what happened the first time Isaac Kaufman was attacked?" cut in Natalie, before they could ramp up their argument. They were getting close to the school and she wanted to hear their take on the situation.

"He was on his way out to his car, same exact route he takes every evening, only this time some guy was waiting for him behind the bushes near the parking lot," said Matt, twisting his bike to the left. "It was the middle of winter, around five o'clock, gets dark really early, so he couldn't see anything. The guy jumped Isaac from behind, started punching and kick-

ing him, smashing his arms and legs with a hockey stick, and yelling that he better keep his mouth shut."

"Wow. How'd you get all the details?"

"This guy Ramiro Lopez, in my civics class, saw it happen."

Natalie shivered. "He watched the whole thing?"

"Nah," said Matt. "When he realized there was no way he could stop the guy, he ran to call the cops. By the time he got back, it was all over."

Natalie nodded gravely. "Thank god someone was around."

"No kidding," said Matt. "Isaac had to be taken to the hospital that time too. Broken arm and stuff."

"No one knows why he was attacked?"

Matt shook his head and led the girls up off the road toward the bike stands. Natalie's stomach sank when she noticed the blondes, standing in the same place as yesterday, sharing a smoke. They were staring straight at her. But Matt's path went right past them and Natalie had no choice but to follow.

The leader opened her mouth to speak. To Natalie's surprise, her voice oozed sweetness. "Good morning, Matthew Hamilton!"

"Hey, Matt!" chorused the sidekicks, tittering. They were totally flirting. Natalie studied Matt's response. His cheeks reddened. Ruth snickered. Clearly, this was a regular routine.

"Hey, Missy. Sandy. Lynette," he said, nodding at each of them in turn.

"Going to the dance on Friday?" asked the one that Matt called Missy.

"Think so."

"Look for me, okay?"

"Sure." Matt hopped off his bike.

As they were locking up, Ruth leaned over to whisper in Natalie's ear: "Missy's talking about the first school dance of the year. She's totally in love with my brother."

Natalie kept her head down, wishing the ground would swallow her whole. She kept expecting the blonde girl to yell out something nasty, something that would embarrass her in front of the Hamiltons. It was unnerving to finally look up and find both siblings staring at her. She realized she'd been in another universe and that Matt had just finished saying something. "Sorry, I missed that. What did you say?"

He swept his hand in an arc to indicate the walls of the nook. "Ramiro Lopez and his buddies did this mural. It's a graffiti transformation project funded by the school." He pointed at a scrawl that looked like it said Ram666. "That's his tag. If you want to know more about what happened, you can pretty much always catch him here after school."

"Thanks," she said, thinking of the guys who'd been here the day before. Surely one of them was Ramiro. "Well, see you later. I'm off to gym class."

"Gym first period!" exclaimed Ruth. "That sucks."

"Tell me about it."

"You're so rude," said Matt to his sister. "You should invite Natalie to eat lunch with you and Suzy. She doesn't know anyone yet."

Ruth looked shy for the first time. "Oh...of course! Want to eat lunch with me and my best friend, Suzy?"

Natalie grinned. "That would be great."

"Meet us in the courtyard out back, where the *surly nerds*

hang out." She banged her brother with her hip and jutted her chin in the direction of the blondes. "Matt never goes out there. He wouldn't want Missy and her friends to think we were infecting him with loser germs."

Matt scowled at his sister. Before he could snap back, Natalie took the opportunity to head to class. She could feel the siblings watching her cross the grass, then risked a quick glance over at the blondes and immediately wished she hadn't. Missy was throwing darts with her eyes.

Behind her, Ruth said to her brother: "Western totally needs a girl like her. Did you see all those earrings? Three in one ear! We are going to be *such* good friends."

"Shut up. She can hear you," Matt whispered, a little too loudly.

Smiling despite herself, Natalie found the girls' gymnasium. A slim, middle-aged woman with bristly gray hair was getting a soccer ball from storage at the far end of the room. According to Natalie's timetable, that would be Ms. Marshall. The teacher greeted her, pointed the way to the change room, and told her to come on out to the field when she was ready. Natalie pushed through the swinging door and settled on an unoccupied section of bench to change into her sweats. There looked to be about twenty-five girls in her class and all of them seemed to know each other.

A couple of minutes later, she laced up her sneakers and headed outside. As she was pushing open the door, she came face to face with Missy and her two friends.

For a second, Missy looked as shocked to see Natalie as Natalie was to see her. Then her face twisted into something much meaner. "How'd you get in here?"

"It's my class."

"I suggest you turn around and go get your timetable changed."

"Why don't you?" Natalie tossed back.

"Trust me. You do not want to be in my gym class," spat Missy, pencil-thin eyebrows arched. With that, she pushed past and entered the change room. Her sidekicks squeezed past too, careful not to touch Natalie.

Ms. Marshall was halfway through breaking the girls into two soccer teams when the blondes came out wearing matching outfits. Natalie was relieved the students weren't picking their own teams, because the fate of the new girl was being chosen last. Her relief soon gave way to panic as she watched the three blondes trade with other students to end up on the opposite team as her when the teacher's back was turned.

Natalie found herself on defence facing Sidekick Sandy on left wing, whose face was twisted into a perma-sneer. Her sparkly eye shadow glinted in the sun. Natalie didn't have time to worry about what they were planning. She got ready to play.

The first skirmish ended when a girl with cornrow braids on Natalie's team gained possession of the ball. She passed to another girl, who sent it flying toward the goal. It was lobbed back onto the field by the opposing team's goalie. The right-winger hit it hard and low. Suddenly, Natalie realized she was standing in front of the net. She leaped sideways and awkwardly managed to block the shot, but fell down onto one knee. The ball arced upward and fell slowly, making it the perfect setup for Sandy, who had plenty of time to kick it straight at Natalie's head and seemed about to do so. Natalie started to

raise her arm, but couldn't stop the ball in time. It slammed into her face and bounced off her cheek.

Stunned, she sank down onto her butt. Tears of humiliation sprang to her eyes. Through them, she could see Sandy laughing, with Missy and Lynette huddled on either side.

"What's your problem?" shouted the girl with braids on Natalie's left.

"Stay out of this, Michelle," warned Missy.

"You wish. I hate bullies."

Ms. Marshall blew a shrill whistle and came running over. "All right, everyone back up." She turned to Natalie. "You okay?"

Natalie touched her cheek. It was hot and sore.

"Sandy and Natalie, see me on the bench. Now!"

Michelle extended a hand to help Natalie up. Her round face was sympathetic.

"She did it on purpose," stammered Natalie.

"Yeah. They always pick on the new kids." Michelle didn't let go of her arm as they walked slowly to the bench, and Natalie was grateful for the support. "They want you to know who's boss around here. Pretty much the entire school is afraid of them."

When they came to the bench, Michelle let go of Natalie's arm so she could go back out to her position on the team. Natalie sat down unhappily. Her cheek was throbbing. Ms. Marshall appeared with a cold pack and placed it gingerly against Natalie's burning cheek. It felt wonderful.

"So what's going on here?" demanded the teacher.

"Nothing," said Sandy sullenly, scuffing a toe of her brand-new white and pink sneakers.

She looked at Natalie. "Do you think 'nothing' just hit you in the face?"

Natalie readjusted the cold pack. "I'm not really sure."

"Well, then, you can both warm this bench for the rest of the period and think about 'nothing.' And Sandy, if 'nothing' ever happens during my class again, you better believe you'll be warming a chair down in the principal's office."

The two girls sat there in silence for the rest of the class. Sandy leaned against the bench and stared straight ahead. Natalie's cold pack gradually got warmer. Praying she wouldn't have a black eye, she went to the change room to check her face in the mirror. It looked red, and she could see the beginnings of a bruise, but no black eye.

She went back outside, and kicked a soccer ball back and forth between her feet, feeling angry and humiliated. When class finally ended, she ran to the change room, threw on her normal clothes and took off for geography. As she passed kids in the hallway, they gawked at her face but didn't say anything. She didn't even spare them a glance.

The geography teacher, Ms. Rahman, also didn't ask any questions, but her eyes kept bouncing back to Natalie's purpling cheek as she handed her a textbook and the class outline she'd missed the day before. She got away from the woman as soon as possible and took a seat under the window. They spent the period going over some basic definitions, then Ms. Rahman gave them a short reading assignment.

Natalie's attention wandered out the window to a clump of guys congregating around a black jeep, listening to drum and bass. She leaned back and focused on the beat vibrating

through her body, letting it wash away her miserable mood. When the lunch bell rang, she sat up with a start. She hadn't even looked at the geography assignment. If the school year continued like this, her grades were really going to suffer.

She gathered her books and trudged outside to find the courtyard where she was supposed to meet Ruth, and discovered it was the same place she'd sat during lunch yesterday. She sank to the ground under the sad little maple tree and pulled out her diary to write while she waited. Minutes later, Ruth burst out of the doors, laughing loudly. Her friend, a tall girl with nerd-queen glasses, was slagging their English teacher's decision to make them read *The Taming of the Shrew* for the second time.

Ruth noticed Natalie sitting alone and came running over, blonde curls flying. A few feet away, she threw herself into a cartwheel. Natalie scooted out of the way at the last second. Ruth landed dangerously close to Natalie's legs, and the diary went flying. It landed open at the other girl's feet. She bent to pick it up and her black hair shone red momentarily when it fell over her face, like a jagged-edged curtain. She handed the book back without glancing at the writing, and Natalie's mood lightened significantly.

"Hi. I'm Suzy Moon," said the girl.

"Natalie Fuentes."

Ruth sat upright and noticed Natalie's bruised cheek. She gasped dramatically. "What happened?"

"Sandy slammed a soccer ball into my face," said Natalie matter-of-factly.

"She's in your gym class?"

Natalie smiled ruefully. "All three of them are. Missy, Sandy, Lynette."

"Ugh."

"They stood there laughing at me after it happened."

Suzy sat down on a flat rock and made the sign of the cross in front of her chest as if to ward off vampires. "Whatever you do, don't show fear. They attack at the first sight of blood."

"No," said Ruth. "Get even and they'll leave you alone for good."

"There's nothing they fear more than being knocked off their pedestals," agreed Suzy. "Sandy's uncle is a teacher at our school, so she gets away with awful stuff all the time."

"Come on, we'll brainstorm revenge plans over grilled cheese," said Ruth, linking arms with Natalie.

"I'm starving," added Suzy. "We always eat at the diner around the corner on Wednesdays. Can't beat the super-cheap grilled cheese special. Two bucks a sandwich."

They walked to the sidewalk and turned down the street.

"You should put green dye in their peroxide," suggested Ruth, out of the blue.

"Or steal their clothes during gym class," said Suzy.

The thought of butting heads with those girls anytime soon wasn't exactly appealing to Natalie. "That would only work if we were swimming. And I doubt they'd let me anywhere near their hair dye."

"*Dye? What dye? It's natural. When I was born, my mother wanted to name me Precious McGoldilocks,*" mimicked Suzy.

Natalie snickered.

"I've got it," said Ruth, slapping her forehead. "Missy's

been in love with my brother since grade six. We've got to be able to use that somehow."

"Hmm. I'd need Matt's cooperation for that and he barely knows me—why should he care?"

"You don't have to ask him—I will," said Ruth, small fists clenched in determination. She threw a few air punches as they entered the diner, a long room with no tables, just a row of stools facing the counter. The cook standing behind it wore a greasy apron. He took their order with a grunt and they sat down.

Their grilled cheese sandwiches came cut up into four triangles, with a single slice of kosher dill pickle on the side. Suzy asked Natalie about yesterday's accident, and whistled when she showed off her bruised arm. "Western hasn't exactly welcomed you, has it? On behalf of the entire school, let me say that I'm truly sorry."

"And we're glad you're here," added Ruth.

"Thanks," said Natalie, blushing. Her emotions were zigzagging all over the place these past couple of days—up, down, up, down. Happy, angry, lonely, embarrassed. It was totally unnerving. Normally, she was a calm person. Right now, she felt stretched thin.

"I wonder how Isaac Kaufman's doing," said Ruth, nibbling on a cheesy triangle.

Natalie hadn't mentioned that she'd been to visit him at the hospital. The girls were surprised to learn she'd managed to get inside the ICU. "He was asleep last night, but the doctors told Jacob his dad was getting better."

"Jacob must be worried," said Ruth.

"Whatever," said Suzy, shaking her head. "He's totally anti-social."

"He reminds me of Seth from *The O.C.*"

Natalie laughed.

Suzy rolled her eyes, stood up and brushed some crumbs off her black jeans. "Come on, crush girl. Time to go. Lunch is almost over."

Natalie extracted her digital camera from her canvas bag. "Wait. Let me take a couple photos first. I'll email them to you." She set the timer and positioned the camera on a nearby window ledge. They put their heads together and posed. She showed the photos to the other girls and was relieved to see the bruise on her cheek wasn't too obvious. While they gawked, she pulled out her diary, opened it to a clean page and jotted down their emails.

"You write in there a lot?" asked Suzy.

"I guess," said Natalie, flipping it shut. "Mostly notes for my zine, *My Very Secret Life*."

"What's a zine?" asked Ruth.

"A little photocopied magazine filled with my own writing and art."

"That's so-o-o cool," said Ruth.

"Hey, speaking of zines, do either of you know a cheap photocopy shop? I need to print up some more copies."

Ruth and Suzy burst out laughing. Natalie looked confused.

"My mother has a couple photocopiers in her office supplies store," confessed Suzy. "It's just a few blocks away from where you live. I can guarantee you a very good deal, if you come over while she's out with my dad at their church group."

"How good?" asked Natalie, pretending to consider the offer.

"The best. A five-finger discount."

"Free photocopies, my favorite kind!"

Suzy wiggled her eyebrows. "Come by tomorrow evening, and I'll hook you up."

"How's eight-thirty—after dinner?"

"Great. You'll have forty-five minutes."

Suzy and Ruth headed off to class. Natalie ran up to her locker to get her textbooks for the afternoon, relaxed and in a good mood for the first time since she'd set foot in this school. She stopped short a few steps from the locker. The blood drained from her face. Spray-painted across the gray metal door were the words: "BACK OFF, NOSY SLUT."

She looked around suspiciously, as if she might discover the perpetrator hanging around in the hall. Who would do this? Sandy and her friends? The attacker? Someone must have seen who did it. At her old school, in New York, there were cameras installed in the hallways. Not here.

A swell of students passed by in either direction. They slowed to stare at the locker, and then at her, but nobody looked particularly guilty. One boy asked, "Who's that?"

His friend answered, "Some new kid."

"The new kids always get it," commented his friend, not caring that she could hear every word.

She made a face at them. They looked away quickly and kept walking.

It could have happened last night, she fumed, because she hadn't gone to her locker before gym or geography this morning. No—it must have happened during lunch, or it would have

been removed. Surely the school wouldn't let graffiti like this stay up long. A caretaker would scrub it off. But Isaac Kaufman was the chief caretaker, and he was in the hospital.

She grabbed her books and slammed the locker shut. In math class, she slid into her seat and hid behind her binder. She didn't look up or speak for the entire class. In English, they started a poetry segment, and Mr. Wallace made them take turns reading poems aloud. When he got to her, she was surprised to hear her voice come out strong and steady. Just as the teacher was starting to analyze Emily Dickinson's unusual punctuation, a P.A. announcement rang out, asking for Natalie Fuentes to come down to the principal's office.

She packed up her stuff and slinked out of the classroom, knowing everyone probably thought she was about to get in trouble. Or maybe they all knew the dismal truth. Gossip spread quickly through a high school. Even with all the strange things happening around here, it couldn't be normal that a new kid witnesses a brutal attack, gets hit in the face by a soccer ball and has her locker defaced within two days. Or maybe it was. Maybe this was exactly why nobody wanted to transfer into the school.

Down in the office, a mousy secretary with a pretty but hesitant smile informed her that Principal Jefferson was on an important phone call and she'd have to wait a few minutes. Natalie sat down and watched the woman work: her blonde hair was carefully styled and she'd taken care with her outfit, a pencil-thin skirt and a floral-patterned blouse. She'd be pretty if it weren't for the horizontal worry lines etched in her forehead and an expression that made her look like a

← mousy secretary

deer caught in headlights whenever a student came in and spoke to her.

It was a full ten minutes before Jefferson's door opened and Natalie was invited into the inner sanctum. The principal shut the door behind them and gestured for Natalie to sit down.

"Hello, Natalie. I spoke to your father this morning. He's concerned about your safety."

"I'm fine."

Jefferson leveled a look at her cheek. "If you're so fine, what's this I hear about being hit in the face by a soccer ball during gym class?"

"It's nothing."

"Highly unlikely. And the locker?"

Natalie looked up. "You know about that?"

"Of course I do. I saw the graffiti."

"Ah."

Jefferson waited for her to speak, but Natalie sat there silently. "Are the other kids picking on you for some reason?"

"Sure. That always happens at a new school."

"Not in my school, it doesn't."

Natalie snorted. "Right."

Jefferson's eyebrows raised. "Not that I'm aware of, anyhow."

"It happens at every school. Trust me."

The principal sighed and pushed her chair back. She went over to an old filing cabinet and unlocked the bottom drawer, marked CONFIDENTIAL. She flipped through folders for a moment, then withdrew one and brought it back to the desk. The name "Sandy Blatchford" was on a label affixed to the top. Natalie was

surprised the school still used paper files. Everything was electronic these days.

Jefferson flipped the folder open and scanned a few pages. "Hmm. Just as I thought. Sandy has already been reprimanded twice. This will make three. According to school regulations, I should suspend her."

"I really don't think you should do that," said Natalie quickly. She'd been peering at the file. The urge to read Sandy's confidential records and find out why she'd been reprimanded before made her fingers itch.

Jefferson closed the folder and pushed it a few inches away. "Give me one good reason."

Um, because her uncle's on your staff, thought Natalie. "Things will only get worse for me."

"They're awfully bad as it is."

"I'm handling it."

Jefferson pinched the bridge of her nose, as if she was trying to ward off a migraine. "Natalie, this school can't handle any more problems. I'm already a black sheep with the school board and...things don't look good. I can't take any chances."

"Just give it a couple more days, Ms. Jefferson. If things haven't improved, I'll be the first one to ask for your help," Natalie said in a rush. "I don't have a problem snitching. I promise. That whole suffer in silence thing's not for me."

"I'll think about it."

"Thank you."

"But you should know that even if these things hadn't occurred, I was going to call you out of class today to apologize for my behavior after the accident. I wasn't acting professionally.

You see, I'm extremely concerned about Isaac Kaufman...and about the future of this school. I should have taken the time to commend you for handling that situation in a very mature way. You may have saved Mr. Kaufman's life. And, contrary to what I said yesterday, I value that kind of initiative among my students."

"Th...thanks," Natalie stuttered, surprised at her reaction. After everything that had happened these past few days, Principal Jefferson's words made tears prickle behind her eyes. She looked up at the ceiling and blinked.

"It's not easy being the new kid, is it?"

Natalie shook her head, biting her lip.

"Look, Natalie, I don't miss much. You can talk to me. Don't forget that."

chapter four

 atalie's emotions were still jangling around like charms on a bracelet when she exited the school from the double doors closest to the office, thinking about whether or not the principal was sincere about wanting to help. The woman's attitude seemed to have shifted 180 degrees.

Natalie found herself next to the staff parking lot. It was just after three-thirty, and already most of the cars were gone. As she circled around to the bike stands, she was highly conscious that this was the exact route Isaac Kaufman had taken—in the opposite direction—when he'd been attacked eight months earlier.

The hair on her neck stood on end as she passed a stretch of bushes that were tall and deep enough for several people to hide in. She heard a noise, or thought she did. Peering around intently, she quickened her pace. No one was in sight.

She rushed to the bike cranny and discovered the same guys working on the mural. The Romeo-in-training who'd annoyed her yesterday lifted his sunglasses and straightened up when he saw her coming. He'd been engrossed in a tête-à-tête with a scruffy-looking friend wearing a cut-off shirt.

Tattoos crept up the other guy's muscular biceps.

"Are any of you named Ramiro Lopez?" she asked.

The tough guy's entire body stiffened. He examined her for a long moment, glanced around, then trotted off to a tricked-up Mazda waiting at the curb.

"Who wants to know, Maggie Chascarillo?" asked Romeo.

"That's not my name," she growled.

"What, no sense of humor?"

That's it. It was time for people to start treating her decently. Right now.

"What," she spat. "Do you think you're the only guy who's told me I look like Maggie? Puhlease. How many punk Latinas are there in comics? Let me help you out: I can count them on my middle finger. And next time you see a cute girl, here's a little tip—if you're going to try some *piropo,* go for something a little less cheesy than the stuffed crust at Pizza Hut."

"It's a compliment," he said, confidence faltering for a second. Then he recovered his bravado and lifted his hands, fingers curled into claws. "Ooh, *la chica* fights back."

She gritted her teeth and looked at each of the boys in turn. "Look, maybe you didn't hear my question. Is Ramiro Lopez around? I need to talk to him."

"Maybe you didn't hear mine: Who wants to know?"

"My name is Natalie Fuentes."

"Tell me why you want to speak to Ramiro, and I'll tell you if he's around."

She rolled her eyes. "Fine. I need to talk to him about the attack against Isaac Kaufman in February. I'm the student who saw what happened yesterday, and I'm wondering if the guy

who broke into Mr. Kaufman's office might be the same one who jumped him before."

He leaned casually on a buddy's shoulder. A thick gold chain with a cross at the end of it swung freely in front of his chest. "Well, Maggie, he's not around right now. So run along and we'll tell him you stopped by. He'll be in touch."

"He has no idea how to find me."

He sucked his teeth, covering up the beginnings of a mischievous grin. "Trust me, Ramiro can find you."

"Whatever," Natalie growled in frustration, shaking her head. She found her diary, ripped out a page, scrawled her email address on it and handed it to the guy. He pocketed it and turned away. The other guys went back to their respective activities, giving her the cold shoulder as a single unit.

She considered informing them that they looked like actors in a Broadway musical, with that big, colorful set behind them. Instead, she just unlocked her bike and rode off.

Her father wasn't home when she got there, but she found a note on the kitchen counter saying he'd be back at dinnertime and would bring food. She made a peanut butter sandwich to tide her over and stomped up to her room, chomping away. It was all right to take out her bad mood on an empty house.

The first thing she did was root around in her cosmetics bag to find a small bottle of concealer that matched her tan skin perfectly. Her Argentine grandmother had taken her on a shopping spree during the summer visit after fretting for several days over the fact that Natalie's mother was too busy to worry about her cosmetics collection. Natalie barely used any of it, except the black eyeliner and the lip gloss. Today it served

a very practical purpose: covering up the bruise on her cheek, so her father wouldn't ask a million questions. She'd convinced herself she didn't want him to know about it for his own good.

Next, she booted up her computer and discovered an email sitting in her inbox from her mother, Brenda, who had a week off and was spending it in a luxury hotel in Paris. Brenda gushed about how much she missed Natalie, and hoped her daughter was settling into Toronto life. She asked about the new school and the house.

Natalie shut down her email program without responding and fired up instant messenger. Her mother was signed in, so she shut that down too. The last thing she wanted to do was pick over the events of the last few days. Her mom would just freak out and start saying that everything was Jorge's fault. Talk about issues. When it came to her mom, Natalie was a serious case.

Natalie considered checking out Jacob's website, but decided that she needed a break from all things Kaufman. She dropped the new Magnetic Fields into her computer's CD player. The band always cheered her up. Their lyrics were more lonely and cynical than she could ever be. Then she opened a box to unpack. Books filled the shelves, her My Little Pony collection went into a cupboard (she still hadn't been able to bring herself to part with it), and the rest of her CDs went into the storage unit. Before she knew it, there weren't any boxes left. It was as if she'd been in a trance, listening to music and letting a sea of thoughts rush through her head while her hands mechanically put things away.

When her father got home, she was sitting on the bed, writing in her notebook. She'd been reading her old copy of

The Nancy Drew Sleuthing Guide, which she'd found at the bottom of a box, and it had brought back memories. She was given the book for her tenth birthday. They were living in London, England, for a few months, while her parents researched a story. Natalie spent her days doing assignments so she wouldn't fall behind the rest of her class back home, and her evenings working through chapters of the book. She analyzed her parents' handwriting, took fingerprints and tracked mysterious footprints around the park near their rental flat.

Now, she tossed her notebook aside and trundled downstairs to see what her father had picked up for supper, prodded by her rumbling stomach. It turned out he'd stopped at an El Salvadoran restaurant recommended by a colleague and brought back a spread of tamales, pupusas and crunchy tacos that made her mouth water. She evaded her dad's questions about school by going on the offensive and asking him about his conversation with Jefferson.

"I spoke to her first thing this morning. She seems to think the attack was an isolated event, that nothing like that will happen again."

He must have spoken to Jefferson before she found out about the soccer ball and the locker graffiti, Natalie realized, or else the principal would have been a little more concerned. But the concealer seemed to be doing its job. Her dad didn't even notice the bruise.

Around eight-thirty, she was doing a little homework when the phone rang. She snatched it up before the second ring. Her dad came on to the upstairs line at the same time and they spoke in unison: "Hello?"

"This is Detective Carl Lewis from 14th Division," boomed a man's voice.

"Hi. It's for me, Dad. He's the one who talked to me after the accident."

"Is everything all right?" demanded her father.

"Yes, sir—"

"I'm Jorge Fuentes, her father."

"Mr. Fuentes, I need Natalie to come down to the station so I can ask her a few more questions."

"Did something happen?" asked Natalie. "Is Isaac okay?"

"As far as I know, Isaac's safely at the hospital, recovering," said Lewis.

"Is it urgent?" asked Jorge.

"As soon as possible would be good."

"We'll be there," said her dad, firmly.

"Sir, I'm afraid you'd just have to wait in the lobby while I talk to your daughter alone."

"I see."

Natalie could tell her dad wasn't happy to hear that.

"Is there anything I should know, then?" asked Jorge, eventually.

"Nope," said Lewis. "See you soon, Natalie."

"Bye," she said.

They all disconnected. When her father came downstairs, he was irritable. The whole way to the police station, he tried to get her to admit she was more involved in this than she was letting on. Her attempts to calm him down were unsuccessful.

Natalie's own mood dampened as they approached the police station. She wasn't looking forward to seeing the

detective she thought of as Linebacker Lewis. It wasn't the man she dreaded, so much as his profession. He'd been perfectly polite up to this point, but you just couldn't grow up visiting war zones without developing a healthy mistrust for people who carried guns.

Her dad parked on the street in front of the imposing block of a building and threw her a warning glance before opening up a magazine to read while he waited. Natalie took her time walking up to the entrance, the only visible way in or out. Tall window slats no more than a hand's span wide—hardly enough to call windows—were too thin for a bolting criminal to fit through sideways, she guessed. She pushed through the glass door and entered a sterile lobby that smelled overpoweringly of bleach. Bleach covering up more organic smells like sweat, blood and urine.

Her boots thunked dully across the linoleum floor. A policeman in full uniform sat behind the registration desk. A sign in front of him read: "Visitors must sign in and present identification." Stacks of paper on the desk gave him an occupied air. So did his stubborn refusal to look up until she cleared her throat right in front of him.

His eyes darted from the top of her head down to her toes, giving her the impression he was assessing whether or not she could be dangerous. She was pretty sure he'd noticed the bruise on her cheek, despite the concealer, but he'd decided her hot pink Le Tigre T-shirt was too girly to signify a troublemaker.

He took his time sipping some coffee from a Styrofoam cup and eased the pinch of his belt around his full belly before drawling: "What can I do for you?"

What was it about cops that made her feel if she did or said anything wrong, she might be arrested? "I'm here to see Detective Lewis. He asked me to come down as soon as I could."

He shifted in his seat and wiped small beads of sweat off his forehead with a soggy napkin. That uniform must be hot. He picked up a phone, paged Lewis, then pushed a clipboard with a stack of forms toward her. "Fill this out."

She jotted down all the necessary information and passed it back.

He skimmed it over, mopping his forehead again. "I.D.," he barked.

She fumbled in her bag to find the brightly colored Guatemalan wallet her mother had given her as a Hanukkah gift, and handed over last year's student card, wondering if he'd notice that it said she still went to Brooklyn Heights. He clipped it to the form without a word, and nodded meaningfully at a bench across the lobby.

Her knee bounced nervously as she perched on the edge of the bench to wait. It was secured to the floor and wall with thick metal bolts. The sooner Natalie could get out of this place, the better.

A steady flow of down-and-out types filed past the front desk. A gaggle of skinny women in tight miniskirts and stilettos hurried out the door to light up cigarettes, cackling about the cop who'd just interrogated them. A meaty officer half-carried a drunk guy who was mumbling slurred curses over to the desk to be booked. Two businesslike policewomen rushed out carrying stacks of file folders and plastic baggies filled with small items. Evidence?

Lewis finally strode through the double doors separating the lobby from the inner sanctum. He was every bit as gigantic as she remembered. When he reached out to shake her hand, his fingers engulfed hers. He managed to apply just enough pressure to let her know she couldn't get loose until he was good and ready. After dropping her hand, he boomed, "We're going to talk in my office."

Gesturing for her to follow, he set off at a brisk pace around the welcome desk, inclined his head toward the guy sitting there and received a grunt in response. The local police force's communication system clearly consisted of head signals and occasional barked commands.

In the back area, narrow aisles separated cubicles in various states of disarray. Uniformed officers ate or picked at keyboards in some of them. Others were empty. Lewis's "office" turned out to be yet another cubbyhole at the far end. Although his had glass walls on three sides, it was barely large enough for a computer terminal, a filing cabinet and an extra chair.

A bulletin board above his desk was covered with newspaper clippings documenting good deeds. There was Lewis brainwashing kids at a local elementary school. Lewis arresting a drunk driver. Lewis looking like a freshly scrubbed Boy Scout as he made a statement to the press about the kidnapping of a local woman.

When he took a seat in his cheap wheelie office chair, she plopped down too. A single picture frame rested on the small desk next to his monitor, but its photo was turned away from her. She strained forward, trying to see the front of the photo, but couldn't.

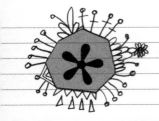

"Thanks for coming down, Ms. Fuentes," said Lewis, twisting his chair so it faced her. "I assume you've heard about the robbery. I'll get right to my questions..."

Natalie held up a hand. "Wait a minute—what robbery?"

His face faltered for an instant, momentarily registered surprise. "It happened at your school tonight, not long before I called you."

"More sports equipment was stolen?" she guessed.

He raised an eyebrow. "Jogged your memory?"

She scrunched up her face. "A lucky guess."

"I'm thinking you might know something about it."

This man was trying hard to get under her skin. "All I know is that things have been disappearing from Western lately—sports equipment and stuff."

He pulled his spiral notepad out of his shirt pocket and flipped through it. "This incident was a little more unsettling than usual."

"How so?"

He hesitated. "Among other things, someone who doesn't like Principal Jefferson decided to let that be known on the auditorium doors."

"High school kids never like their principals."

"A threat, Natalie," he snapped. "Saying the truth will come out and, when it does, she's going to get canned."

"Oh." He was saying someone wanted Jefferson fired?

He crossed his hands in front of his chest. "Look, now's the time for you to give me any additional information that's come to mind since we talked yesterday."

She tried to remember something—anything—new to tell

him about the attack. Nothing came to mind, so she decided to start from the very beginning. "Well, I took a shortcut into the school because some girls were picking on me."

He flipped through his notepad again. "Melissa Waddell, Sandy Blatchford and Lynette Duchamp?"

"Right. At least, I guess those are their last names."

"Then what happened?" he asked.

"I heard two men shouting when I passed Mr. Kaufman's office."

"Do you remember what they were saying?"

She made a big show of pausing to wrack her brain. "Just a bunch of swearing and I think I heard the attacker tell Isaac to keep his mouth shut."

"Why would he say that?"

"I have no idea!" she said. "All I know is that people seem more interested in what I was doing in that hallway than in catching whoever's behind the attack."

"We're trying to catch the guy, Natalie. I'm investigating several avenues." He sat back and changed topics abruptly. "Ms. Fuentes, why do you think Mr. Kaufman's computer was smashed?"

"How would I know?"

He pushed his chair back suddenly. "Associating with known criminals like Jacob Kaufman doesn't give me much confidence in your judgment."

Oh, right. According to Jacob's online essay, Fourteenth Division was where they'd taken him when he was arrested. "You think Jacob attacked his own father?"

"Of course not."

"Then what do you mean?"

"It means I think there's more to this situation than it seems."

"Well, maybe if you gave me a little information, I wouldn't have to walk around expecting the 'situation' to hit me in the face at any moment."

"This is a *police investigation,*" he intoned like a mantra. "Our information isn't available to the general public. You are a member of the general public who found herself in the wrong place at the wrong time. I suggest you stay away from Jacob and Isaac until the attacker has been brought to justice."

"Easy for you to say," Natalie muttered under her breath.

He didn't respond, just stood up and stepped out of the cubicle. Seeing no other alternative, she trailed after him to the lobby, where he informed the officer on duty she was free to go, then disappeared without saying goodbye.

She got her student I.D. back, went outside and got into her dad's car. As they drove away, he asked her how it went. She responded distractedly, consumed by the thought it might not be long before the cops accused her of helping Isaac's attacker, and possibly also commiting a string of other crimes.

Back at home, she flipped on the television and pretended to be engrossed in whatever was on. Whenever her mind wandered back to Isaac Kaufman, she got upset all over again. She felt responsible, since she'd found him lying on the floor. If she'd intervened sooner, maybe he wouldn't have been hurt.

Despite Lewis's warning, she was more determined than ever to figure out what was going on at her new school. And that included getting the blondes to leave her alone, which

would take a little preparation. She wouldn't be able to handle it tomorrow. The easiest thing was to skip gym class until she was properly prepared. As she drifted off to sleep, her last conscious thought was about how Sandy managed to look cute and mean at the same time. If you asked her, those girls were entirely nasty enough to commit some kind of heinous crime.

Chapter five

T hursday morning sunlight crashed through the east-facing windows of her room and woke Natalie up in the middle of a dream. She'd been back in the old Brooklyn apartment, before things got really bad between her parents. The three of them were lounging on the couch, watching the evening news like they did every night.

Suddenly the scene had shifted. Her parents faced off at either end of the couch, screaming over her head about whose turn it was to walk the dog. Brenda got louder and more emotional in response to Jorge withdrawing. Both of them were ignoring Natalie, who was caught in the middle, trying to shut out their screaming by covering her ears with her hands. Brenda threatened to call the cops if Jorge didn't take the dog to the park. She wound back her arm to whip the leash at his head just when Natalie's eyes popped open.

She lay there in bed, blinking, disoriented by the fact that her family had never owned a dog. When she finally realized it was a dream, she groaned loudly and burrowed down into the pillows. Unfortunately, her stomach was rumbling insistently.

She gave up on sleep and threw back the comforter with a dramatic sigh. It felt like she was starring in a bad B-movie

called *Betrayal Of The Fifty-Foot Parental Units* or maybe *Attack Of The Killer Blondes*. She swung her legs off the bed and pulled on a jean skirt and a T-shirt, thinking she should start screen-printing her own slogan shirts with fake movie posters on them.

When she left the house to head to school, she found Ruth and Matt waiting outside. She told them to go on without her, that she was skipping gym class. As the Hamiltons rode off, Natalie scanned the front windows of her house to make sure her dad wasn't watching, then dragged her bike around to the side walkway. Putting on her MP3 player, she sat down on the ground to wait. Once he'd driven off, she ran back inside and went up to her room, where she turned on her computer and surfed over to Jacob's website to pass the time.

The front page was a collection of short news items he found interesting. Most of them were about ownership of Internet companies and had comments written underneath them by people with nicknames like "Someguy," "Ghost" and "Spider." The most recent item was about a hacker who'd managed to read the U.S. Secret Service's email for over a year. She logged in under the username "Natalia" and posted a quick response to let him know she'd stopped by.

Next, she clicked on the Info page. There, she found a profile of Jacob's face drawn entirely out of ASCII letters (it was virtually impossible to tell it was him) and a couple of sentences next to it: "After being educated the hard way about security on the Internet, Jacob Kaufman decided he needed to figure out what the people who'd had him arrested were able to see. The publisher of the online magazine *The*

Anarchives, he's also known as a Toronto high school student."

At that point, it was almost ten, so she took off for school and discovered that someone had painted the bike stand with heavy black paint overnight. It was more than a little disconcerting to lock up to an enormous black banana. She swung by the auditorium doors to see if the threat to Jefferson was still there, but they'd been scrubbed clean.

Avoiding her locker, she headed straight to geography. Half a dozen students dotted the room when she arrived. Just as she was about to take her place under the window again, she noticed that Jacob was sitting at the back of the room, hunched over the short reading they'd been assigned during yesterday's class. She zigzagged through the desks and tapped him on the shoulder.

"Hey," he said.

"You're not surprised to see me."

"I already knew you were in this class."

"How, exactly?"

His eyes glinted. "I have my ways."

She wiggled spirit fingers. "Ooh. The mysterious computer hacker is investigating me."

His jaw dropped.

"You didn't think I knew about your sordid past, did you?"

"Well, to be honest, how do you?"

She slipped into a seat across the aisle from him. "Easy. I Googled you."

"Ahh. The joys of living under a global monitoring system."

She opened her bag and took out her binder. "How's your father doing?"

"Better—much better, actually. They're releasing him this afternoon."

"Already?"

"Yeah, I'm going to get him after school. Hospitals like to free up beds as soon as possible."

"Not in the States. They keep you there forever, to run up your bill."

The classroom door opened, and Ms. Rahman entered, followed by a flood of students who had clearly been stalling in the hallway until the very last second. Natalie didn't have an opportunity to ask any more questions.

Natalie noticed Jacob scribbling something on a piece of paper. He folded it into a small square and tossed it onto her desk while the teacher was writing notes on the blackboard.

She opened it:

Need to talk. Meet me in the hallway near my dad's office after school. — J

She wrote that she'd be there and passed it back to him. He read her response and nodded curtly, lips compressed. For the rest of the class he faced forward, giving every impression of being completely engrossed in the fluvial erosion that had formed the Canadian Shield thousands of years ago. When the period ended, he collected his books and rushed off with a quick nod.

Natalie made her way out to the courtyard to find Ruth and Suzy for lunch. Suzy gave Natalie the rundown on their weekly schedule while they walked to World's Best Falafel House: "Monday's bagged, Tuesday's bagged, Wednesday's cheap grilled cheese, Thursday's a $2 falafel special, and Friday's

either bagged or veggie subs, depending on our mood."

"Sure," said Natalie, preoccupied by Jacob's request.

Ruth studied her, eyebrows knit in concern. "I'm afraid to ask what's up."

"I heard the P.A. announcement yesterday," added Suzy, before Natalie could respond. "Did Jefferson bawl you out or something?"

"No. She was actually really nice. Played the supportive principal role. It's just...well, have you been to the gymnasium lately?"

"Yeah, we had gym last period yesterday," said Ruth.

"Did any of the lockers look weird to you?" She winced.

"That's your locker?" asked Suzy.

"Uh-huh."

"No wonder you didn't go to gym this morning," said Ruth. "It's probably been cleaned off by now, though. The school never lets graffiti stick around for long."

"I haven't been able to bring myself to go up there since I first saw it," Natalie admitted.

"I'll check it out and let you know how it looks after school," said Ruth. "I bet Missy and her pals had something to do with it. I mean, it was hot pink paint, right?"

"Now you definitely have to get even," said Suzy, jaw set. "Those girls must be taken down."

"I'm not sure if it was the Golden Girls or the attacker. But I've got a plan to deal with Missy. It involves Matt. Can you arrange for him to meet me somewhere private after school?"

"Sure," said Ruth. "How about my garage?"

"I'll be there too," said Suzy.

"If your parents let you get away from the shop," qualified Ruth.

Suzy looked stumped for a moment, then her face brightened. "I won't miss this, even if I have to lie and say I'm going to the library to work on a project with some kids from science class. Trust me, I can get away with anything if my parents think I'm a keener. They'd be happy if I studied 24-7, even during the summer."

Ruth groaned. "The only thing my mother cares about is my dance class—and that's just to make sure I'm not totally screwing up."

As Ruth and Suzy chattered away about their respective family woes, Natalie decided it was nice having partners in crime. She made a mental note to thank her father.

After lunch, she avoided her locker again. Since nothing traumatic had happened that day, she was beginning to feel like a normal student. When English ended, she went downstairs and found Jacob sitting on the floor, leaning against a wall near the door to the hallway leading to his dad's office. His knees were pulled up and his laptop rested on them. He was typing. When he saw her coming, he shut the computer.

"You found my website," he said, eyes signalling respect.

"Yep."

He stood up. "Cool. Thanks for posting."

"No problem."

He pulled a Homer Simpson key chain out of his pocket and opened the locked door.

"Does your dad know you have that key?"

"Of course," he said, heading down the hall to the office

door and using a key to open that too. "I practically grew up here. My mother died when I was six years old, so my dad was a single parent. I've spent P.D. days and most after-school hours in this office."

She followed him down the stairs and looked around. The back half of the room was still a mess, but now a thin film of white powder from the fingerprinting process covered everything too. The computer had been returned to the desk, and a different monitor was connected to it.

"Does that thing still work?" she asked.

Jacob shook his head. "Nah. Thought I'd test it out, just to see. I'll probably be able to salvage some of the parts. Not sure about the hard drive."

She walked over to the metal cupboard. A shiver passed down her spine. "The guy was hiding inside this. He jumped out when I was trying to call for help." She turned the knob on one of the doors and pulled it open. Instead of being empty, as she'd expected, this half was overflowing with stacks of paper and newspaper clippings. Pretty strange, considering the rest of the caretaker's office was filled with neatly arranged work supplies.

"Was your dad working on something? A project?"

Jacob shrugged. "He collects anything that mentions Western. Been doing it for years."

Natalie pulled a folded section of newspaper out from under a stack. Dated a couple of months ago and buried at the back of the front section, it was a *Star* article about Western's disappearing sports equipment. She put it away and picked another randomly. It was a profile of the school's beloved

football coach, Mr. Marsden, who'd held the position for more than twenty years before retiring.

She tugged open the other side of the cupboard, but it was just a makeshift closet, with hooks for coats and a spare pair of green overalls that matched the ones Isaac Kaufman had been wearing when she found him.

"My dad really wants to meet you," said Jacob suddenly. "He's very grateful. Says you saved his life."

Natalie didn't respond. They both knew it was all too possible.

"He invited you for dinner. We don't live far."

"Tonight?" Her schedule was getting full. "Sure, but I have to go home first." She decided not to mention her appointment with Ruth, Suzy and Matt. If she didn't want to skip gym class forever, she had to deal with that situation as quickly and quietly as possible.

His face lit up. "That's great. My dad's convinced something else is going to happen and that you might be able to help him. I'm worried he won't let himself relax and get better until this situation's cleared up. If you come about six-thirty, you can eat with us. My dad'll probably go to sleep early."

"I'll be there."

Jacob gave her the address. They went back up the stairs and he locked the office door behind them.

"Hey, have the cops called you lately?" she asked.

He shook his head. "That detective said he was going to come by and question my father sometime today. I'll probably find out all about it when I bring him home."

They exited from the hallway to the cranny where Natalie's bike was locked. The guys doing graffiti were back again.

The one who'd bothered her the day before raised a hand in greeting when he saw Jacob.

"Hey, man," he said, then he glanced at Natalie and a corner of his mouth tilted up. "Hey, Maggie. Good to see you again."

"Maggie?" asked Jacob, in confusion.

"A *Love and Rockets* character," said Natalie. "This guy thinks he's a real joker."

Jacob quirked his head to one side. "Leave her alone, Ramiro."

"Ramiro?" exclaimed Natalie. "*You're* Ramiro Lopez?"

"I told you yesterday—depends who's asking," said Ramiro, holding up his hands to indicate he was innocent. "Peace, man, I never knew she was with you."

"I'm not *with* him," spat Natalie. "We're just friends."

Ramiro winked at her. "Well, any *friend* of Jacob's is a friend of mine."

"I wanted to ask you some questions about the first attack on Jacob's dad."

He rested one hip against a huge metal apple. "I know what you wanted."

"Right. Well, do you remember anything specific about the guy you saw in February?"

Ramiro thought hard for a second. It looked painful. He made an exaggeratedly clueless face. "Nah. Nothing comes to mind."

"Oh, please."

"Look, Ramiro, you can trust her," said Jacob. "I do."

"In that case—maybe I do remember some things."

"Like..." prompted Natalie.

"Like he was tall. Taller than him," he said, indicating one of his friends, a beanpole of a guy who was right at that moment stretching to add a line of black paint to the graffiti mural. "Wider, too."

"Could've been the same guy," she said. "My guess is he was about six feet."

"Sounds about right."

"Huh. What was he wearing?"

"A hoodie and a black face mask."

"You mean a ski mask?"

"Nah. Some kind of thin black material. Stretchy."

"Any other details? Shoes, or...or jewelry? The guy I saw had on some kind of fancy watch."

"It was too dark to see much," said Ramiro. Natalie guessed he didn't have anything more to add, as he was already turning back to the mural.

"Well... thanks. I guess I'd better get going."

Natalie unlocked her bike and pedaled slowly down to the street with Jacob, who walked beside her. When they were out of earshot, she said: "You and Ramiro seem tight."

"He owes me huge. My dad caught him and his buddies bombing the school walls one too many times. Jefferson was all set to suspend them, thanks to the school board's new zero tolerance rules. Three strikes and you're out. But I got my dad to convince her to put their energy into something legal instead."

"That mural," she guessed. "It was your idea?"

He grinned slyly. "Better than a blank wall, don't you think?"

Natalie rode away, laughing over the fact that Jacob had

convinced Jefferson to sanction a graffiti mural on the school to deter ugly tagging. The best part of his plan is that it would actually work better and be cheaper than installing security cams or scrubbing the walls every time they were bombed with a new tag.

She looked forward to meeting his father. She could finally find out what happened just before he was attacked. What would an observant Jewish caretaker who'd raised a hacker son be like? Janitors were usually the invisible ones. Students ignored them and teachers bossed them around.

Besides, maybe she'd even get to see Jacob's computer system—a hacker's private shrine to technology. And maybe he'd give her his theory about why his dad's computer was specifically targeted.

Back home, she carried her bike up onto her front porch and quietly entered. The phone was flashing to say there was a new message. She listened to it. A recorded message came on: "This is Western High's automated attendance system. A student with the initials N.F. was absent from one or more classes today. Please ensure that this student brings a signed letter to the office before attending this class again."

That was close! Her school in New York didn't automatically call home when you missed a single period. Yeesh. She deleted it, hung up and rushed into the kitchen, where she grabbed an apple and glanced at the clock on the stove. She was late for the meeting.

She slipped the apple into a pocket and headed for the back door. That's when she heard her father's voice coming from the basement.

an apple a day...

...keeps the "close-calls" away!

"Nati? Is that you?"

"Yeah," she yelled. "But I'm on my way out again."

Footsteps sounded on the stairs. He was heading up. "Is everything all right?"

She practically leaped across the room and yanked open the door. "Can't talk now, Dad. Going next door to meet with Ruth and Matt. School stuff."

"Nati, hang on a moment. I spoke to your principal this afternoon..."

She pretended she couldn't hear him, slammed the door behind herself and sprinted through the backyard. A light was on in the Hamiltons' garage. Hooking a leg over the chain-link fence between the two houses and hopping it, she kept expecting her father to follow her outside at any moment. She burst into the garage and came to an abrupt halt at the sight of Matt, Ruth and Suzy staring up at her, sitting on wooden fold-out chairs arranged in a circle. An empty seat was waiting for her, so she took it.

"Wow, this is a real council of war!"

"We were just starting to wonder what happened," said Suzy, "'cause I have to be home in half an hour. My mom needs me to watch the store at five-thirty. If I'm a minute late, she'll disown me."

Natalie grimaced. "Sorry. Jacob needed to talk to me. His father's invited me over tonight."

"Wow," said Ruth. "I don't know *anyone* who's been to the Kaufmans' house. You have to tell me *everything* when you get to Suzy's store tonight."

"Jacob's wack," said Matt, grimacing. "He was in my phys

ed class last year and spent more time on the sidelines playing with his laptop than doing any of the sports. I think he deliberately tried to get benched."

"I can understand that," said Natalie ruefully.

"Yeah—not all of us are mega-jocks," said Suzy.

"So, how do we get back at the Golden Girls?" asked Ruth.

"We're not..." said Natalie.

"But they hit you in the face!" said Ruth, perplexed.

"And called you a slut!" added Suzy, crossing her arms in a huff.

"We're not positive they were the ones who spray-painted my locker," said Natalie. "Maybe it was whoever attacked Isaac."

"Of course it was them," said Ruth. "And things will get worse if we don't do something."

"I didn't say I wasn't going to do anything, I said we're not going to get even. We're going to distract them." Natalie turned to look at Matt and sucked in a deep breath, screwing up her courage. "Matt, what do you think of Missy?"

"She's kind of hot," he said frankly, then rushed to add: "But I can't believe she did those mean things to you."

"Believe me, it's not just Natalie she's done mean stuff to," said Ruth.

"Do you like her enough to ask her out?" Natalie asked him.

"I dunno."

"Because I have a serious hunch she'd say yes."

He looked surprised. "What?"

His sister threw her hands up impatiently. "Oh, please. Don't pretend that the Queen Bitch isn't practically throwing herself at you every morning!"

"I heard her rating your butt once," admitted Suzy. "She gave it a nine and a half out of ten."

Ruth snickered. Matt blushed, all the way to the roots of his blond curls. Natalie felt a little sorry for him. His thoughts were so openly displayed on his face. Despite Natalie's aversion to sports and the guys who were obsessed with them, Matt Hamilton was a sweetie.

"Oh noooo," groaned Ruth. "If they start dating, she'll be over at our house all the time and I'll have to be polite to her."

"We all know that politeness thing's so hard for you," joked Suzy.

"You don't understand. I went to elementary school with her. In grade five, she went around telling everyone I still wet my bed. I felt sick to my stomach for two weeks, until she moved on to some other victim. I'm convinced there are still people at our school who think I have a serious problem."

"Why didn't you tell me?" asked Matt. "I would have taken care of it."

She raised an eyebrow and opened her mouth, presumably getting ready to give him an earful. Unexpectedly, she shut it again and all that came out was: "I don't need my brother to take care of me."

"I do," said Natalie, and they all laughed. "While you're out on said date with Missy, you could throw in a good word for me."

"Fine, I'll do it," agreed Matt.

"The supreme sacrifice," teased Suzy.

"One made for the greater good," added Natalie.

Just then, Suzy opened up her pack and took out a binder. She flipped to a blank page and started scribbling ran-

dom words on it, continuing to write until she filled two full pages. Neither Ruth nor Matt seemed to think this was odd.

"What *are* you doing?" Natalie finally blurted out.

"My mother's going to want to check up on the work I did at the library."

"But you're writing garbage!"

She waved a hand. "Don't worry, she won't actually read it. She just checks that I've used my time productively. I need something down on paper that I can wave from a distance."

The three of them watched her write, thinking the same thing—thank god their parents weren't this obsessive about their schoolwork.

"I've got to go get yelled at myself," said Natalie, wincing. "I ran away from my dad just as he was starting to tell me about a conversation he had with Jefferson today. And that's after he freaked when we got a phone call from the cops last night, asking me to come in for more questioning. Everyone seems convinced I'm somehow involved in the weird things happening at Western."

"Aren't you?" asked Ruth.

Natalie wiggled her eyebrows conspiratorially.

Suzy clapped her binder shut and threw it back into her bag. "We'll leave together, then."

They piled their chairs in a corner of the garage and traipsed across the lawn. Natalie jumped the fence and said a quick goodbye before heading inside. Her dad was back in the basement, so she headed downstairs to make peace.

"Sorry for running out before," she said. "I was late meeting the Hamiltons."

He acknowledged her apology with a sniff. "You're starting to worry me, Nati. I've never known you to run away when I'm talking to you!"

"I said I was sorry."

"You're acting so strangely."

"It's not my fault," she protested. "Strange things are happening to *me*."

"At your age, I thought I was invincible."

"I know, Dad," she said. He was clearly remembering his involvement with the rebel movement in Argentina. "But this really doesn't compare to your experience."

"It does. Someone put Isaac Kaufman in the hospital. Principal Jefferson told me about the threat on your locker. And you've been questioned by the police. I can't stop you from being you, I just hope you'll be a little more careful."

"I am careful," she said.

He looked skeptical. "If I hear anything more...unsettling... we're going to have to consider finding you a new school. Mrs. Hamilton told me today that she and her husband have been thinking of transferring their kids out of Western."

Natalie was curious to discover she didn't particularly like the idea of switching schools. The Hamiltons, Suzy and Jacob already felt like friends, even though it had only been a few days.

"Don't you think you're overreacting a little?"

He grunted, but didn't say anything, which she took to mean he wasn't going to make any immediate decisions, but the conversation wasn't over.

"One more thing," she said, hesitantly. "I'm going to the

Kaufmans' for dinner. Isaac's been released from the hospital and wants to thank me in person."

Jorge's face expressed his displeasure, but he didn't try to discourage her from going. Natalie chose to interpret his silence as consent, and went back upstairs before he could change his mind.

chapter six

he Kaufmans' house was shorter than hers, just two floors, but brick as well. Typical Toronto style. She headed up to the door and rang the bell.

Jacob pulled it open seconds later, as if he'd seen her approach.

"C'mon in."

She stepped into the front hall and did a double-take. Lining the walls were rows and rows of tiny ceramic figurines, posed in familiar scenes. They passed mini tableaux of Robin Hood and his Merry Men making camp deep in Sherwood Forest, the animals from Uncle Remus's Brer Rabbit stories acting out the Tar Baby fable, and what looked like the Greek god Zeus wielding his thunderbolts, holding court on a cloud.

She glanced into the living room as they passed it. The figurines dominated the entire first floor.

"You can close your mouth now," said Jacob, smirking. "My dad makes them. It's his hobby. He reads folk tales from all around the world, and modifies premade molds to create the bodies, then paints them by hand."

"They're incredible." Natalie reached out toward an old crone that looked like Baba Yaga, hovering near the obedient

Vasilisa the Beautiful. A picture of them would make the best cover for her zine...

Jacob put a warning hand on her arm. "Don't touch. He'll freak."

She pulled away, shoved her hand in a pocket. "Sorry!"

"Don't worry about it. He has a mild case of OCD. Notices whenever his figurines are moved even a fraction of an inch."

He led her into a cozy, well-used kitchen painted a warm red color. There were only two figurine shelves in there—above the cookbooks and above the door to a room at the back of the house.

Isaac sat in a hard-backed wooden chair at the head of the table with a dramatic bandage around his head. A few locks of white hair had managed to escape from under the bandage and he had dark smudges under his brown eyes. He struggled up from his chair and held out a hand for her to shake. His fingers rested lightly on hers for the briefest moment.

"So this is the lovely young woman who saved my life. I owe you a great debt."

"All I did was call the ambulance," she said, acutely conscious she hadn't intervened in time to stop the actual attack because she'd been worried about getting in trouble.

"If you hadn't been in that hallway, I wouldn't be sitting here today," pronounced Isaac, touching the bandage on his head to accentuate his point.

She tried not to show how much his words disturbed her.

"What did you see, Natalie? Tell me everything."

"Let her sit down first before we grill her," said Jacob.

Natalie took her seat and studied Jacob's father covertly. He wasn't as old as he'd first appeared. Probably in his early sixties, she decided. Maybe it was the after-effects of the head injury, but he seemed worn down. It was hard to imagine anyone deliberately hurting him.

"I made dinner. Don't expect anything fancy," said Jacob, sliding into a chair in front of a lidded dish filled with what looked like cheesy macaroni. Also on the table was a salad with some kind of creamy dressing and soggy green beans.

"Who doesn't love mac and cheese?" said Natalie, forcing excitement into her voice. Jacob served himself and his father, then passed her the dish. She scooped a generous serving of gooey noodles onto her plate.

As the teenagers ate, Isaac Kaufman pushed the food around his plate. Natalie recounted what happened for the fiftieth time. When she told him about the door being propped open, he dropped his head into his hands. "It was my own fault... I leave it open sometimes so air can circulate. It's so musty in the basement..."

"It's not your fault, Dad," protested Jacob.

"You don't know!" said Isaac, lifting his head. "He was just waiting for another opportunity."

"Do you have any idea who did this, Mr. Kaufman?" asked Natalie.

"Call me Isaac." His eyes burned fiercely. "And I've made my fair share of enemies."

"Huh?" she said stupidly.

"I don't stand for any monkey business. Not from the principal. Not from the school board superintendent. Not from the teachers. When we receive supplies I make sure every last item that's been allocated to us is there. Not a single goalpost less."

Natalie served herself some salad and speared a mouthful. "Is that a concern?"

"Oh, yes. You have to watch those shipments. What can you do with a chalkboard if you have no chalk? A computer with no mouse? Useless."

"I see. Mistakes regularly happen?"

"Not mistakes."

"You think someone deliberately skims items from Western's supply orders?"

He inclined his head and munched a tomato thoughtfully.

Jacob looked annoyed, as if he'd heard this theory way too many times. "Dad, we've been through this a million times. The school board can only issue supplies they have in stock. That's why you don't get everything you order."

Isaac snorted. "Yes, but sometimes it's *after* the shipment has arrived that things go walking. That's why I keep a list of every single item."

"On the computer that was smashed?" asked Natalie.

Jacob jumped in. "Nah. It's safe on a centralized server downtown. I created a database that's remotely accessible from any terminal, if you have the right software and a password."

"I see." It was a long shot, but maybe the database had something to do with the attack.

Isaac prodded Natalie. "Keep talking, girl. What happened next?"

She told him the rest of the story, stopping once in a while to clarify what the man looked like and where he'd been hiding. Isaac was particularly interested in the guy's watch, because it was the only personal thing either of them had seen.

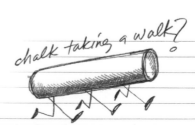
chalk taking a walk?

He made Jacob fetch a pen and paper so she could sketch it. Natalie's drawing abilities left a great deal to be desired. After she handed it over, Isaac shook his head impatiently to say he didn't recognize it.

She wanted to ask about the newspaper clippings in his cupboard, but wasn't sure how to do it without divulging that she and Jacob were poking around. "Isaac, I noticed you've kept newspaper articles about Western over the years. Are you collecting them for some reason?"

"How did you find those?" he asked.

"The day of the attack, the doors were open…"

"They're my private papers." He shrugged. "I'm proud of my school and keep copies of everything that's been written about it, dating back twenty years."

Natalie thought that was a little strange, but she felt guilty about snooping, so she didn't press the issue. Instead, she steered the conversation to his art. "Your figurines are amazing."

He waved away her compliment and leaned forward conspiratorially. "My son tells me you have a way of poking around and finding things out."

She glanced at Jacob, who was munching on a big piece of lettuce, trying to look innocent.

"I Googled you too," Jacob said. "I read all about the time you foiled those purebred dognappers in Brooklyn. And how this summer you helped your father track down a member of Argentina's military junta who was in hiding, so he could be tried by the country's supreme court. Didn't your dad get some kind of award for that?"

"Well, um…" she stammered.

"Seems like unusual situations fall in your lap a lot."

"This is good news," said Isaac. "You can help me. The police are useless. They come here to my house and spend more time looking at my art and Jacob's computer than listening to my theories about the crime. They think I'm a crazy old man. June Jefferson, she doesn't have the guts to press this issue with her boss. Plus, she finds my organizational techniques more than a little... irritating. I've got the eagle eye." He chuckled and peered intently at Natalie. "And that Mike Wojcik. Bah! I wouldn't trust that man far enough to throw a quarter. It's never sat well with him that a lowly caretaker has real power at Western." He slammed the tabletop with a fist, causing his plate to jump. "You and my son must find out who is doing this, before someone succeeds in killing me."

On that final note, Isaac pushed himself up on wobbly arms and started to clear the table. Although he was strong of spirit, he was still weak on his feet. No sooner had he picked up the plate in front of him than he dropped it on the floor and it smashed into a million pieces. Isaac's face collapsed into a mass of worry lines. Natalie looked away, embarrassed to be witnessing his weak moment.

Jacob leaped up and got a broom and dustpan. Without saying anything, Isaac shuffled off into the other room. Jacob's eyes trailed after his father as he swept up the glass.

Natalie wished she could hug him. "The accident really took a toll on your dad, didn't it?"

"He's usually a pretty fit guy. I've never seen him like this, not even when Mom was sick," he said hoarsely.

What could she say? "He'll get better," she murmured.

"He just needs time." He didn't respond. They finished clearing the table in silence.

"Want to see my computer setup?" asked Jacob.

"Sure." She followed him up a narrow flight of stairs, thinking that Jacob was doomed to be an outsider, just like her. Both of them had lived through things other people wouldn't be able to comprehend. He'd watched his mother die. She'd traveled all over the world and had unbelievable experiences because of her parents' jobs. Some things put petty school dramas into perspective.

His room was sparsely furnished. It contained a single bed and a bookcase full of well-thumbed science fiction novels, a few zines and comics. But his desk was the room's real focal point. Natalie counted three computer boxes surrounding it. Two enormous monitors sat side by side on top, and when Jacob touched a button, they turned on. The windows and program icons on the monitors were completely foreign to Natalie.

"So what happened to your mom?" Natalie asked, unable to think of a less blunt way to phrase the question.

"She died. Of cancer," he said, claiming the chair in front of his desk, a plush recliner.

"Oh, I'm sorry."

"I barely remember her. I was only six. How come you decided to live with your dad?"

"Huh? Oh, my mother and I don't get along that well."

"Why not?" He cranked up the footrest, and rested his keyboard on his lap.

She hesitated, then took a seat on the bed and curled her

feet up under her body as she tried to think how to explain such a complicated situation to a person who'd lived his entire life in one place, in one house. During the divorce, her mom had cried all the time for about six months, and kept saying she was fine. But that wasn't really it.

"She's super focused on her work, the people she's writing about, their emergencies. Forgets about her own needs. Forgets that her family needs her too. Forgets about anything other than the latest assignment."

"And your dad?"

She thought for a moment. "He used to be the same as my mom, but he seems to be trying these days. He took a full-time job at the *Toronto Star*—that's why we moved here. We get along all right. He mostly leaves me alone."

"Your parents sound sick."

"Kinda," she said.

"My dad's just a caretaker."

She snorted. "Please. He's a talented artist with a secure job. And I don't see him dragging you around the world every couple months. He's stable. Not like my parents."

A miserable look flashed over his face. "He hasn't touched his work since returning from the hospital. He just sits in the back room, staring out the window."

"He'll get back to it when he's feeling stronger," she assured him. Natalie glanced meaningfully at the computer monitors in order to lessen their conversation's intensity. "I don't recognize any of the programs you're running."

"That's because it's a Linux box." He turned back to his computer to give her a demo. "All the programs I run on it are free too. It's all about being an alternative to corporate software like Microsoft's Windows."

It turned out Jacob was running an Internet server out of his room, using it to power his website, the *Anarchives* database of articles, some newsgroups and a couple of friends' sites. He definitely seemed to know his way around computer networks, she thought, as he clicked onto his website and demanded that she change her nickname. "'Natalia' is too obvious. The idea is to make people guess who you really are. How about 'Gnat,' like the insect?"

"Thanks a lot," she said. "Now I know how annoying you think I am."

He laughed, and some of the stress seemed to flow out of him.

It was drizzling when she finally left the Kaufmans' and rode west through the puddles toward Suzy Moon's store. The sun was setting in front of her: a toxic city palette closer to yellow and green than red and orange. Her hair gradually got wetter and wetter, until she could feel water dripping down her back. She almost didn't mind because of the weird view. Besides, her mind was crowded with thoughts of Jacob and his father.

From outside, Moon Office Supplies looked like every other neighborhood postal counter and stationery store. There was a sign above the door advertising the services of Jerry Moon, chartered accountant. Suzy's dad? Through the front window, Natalie could see shelves packed with paper and padded envelopes. Something above the door dingled when she pushed it open—she assumed it was a bell, but it turned out to be two

gnat (na⁻t)\
n.

Any of various small, biting, two-winged flies, such as a punkie or black fly.

[Middle English, from Old English *gnæt*.]

small, naked metal cherubs that danced around and bounced off each other.

Suzy was behind the counter, reading a textbook. She looked up and her jagged hair swung off her face. Anticipating a customer, her face was already frozen in a polite grin. Seeing Natalie, it melted into a more normal expression.

"Finally!" said Ruth, jumping up. Natalie hadn't seen her at first, but she was sitting on a low stool off to the side of the counter, reading a copy of *People* magazine.

"Suzy said eight-thirty," responded Natalie, feeling a little irritable because she was soggy. Plus the girl was irrationally cheery all the time.

"I know, but I'm dying to hear *everything*," said Ruth, sounding a little frantic.

Suzy reached into a drawer behind the counter and pulled out a Xerox key chain. Natalie opened her bag and took out the originals of three issues of *My Very Secret Life*. She didn't feel completely comfortable gossiping to Suzy and Ruth right after meeting Jacob's dad. He'd trusted her with some personal information and Ruth didn't seem particularly discreet.

"Let her get the photocopies set up first," said Suzy, as if she was reading Natalie's mind. "My parents will be back in an hour."

"Fine," said Ruth, pouting.

The door jingled and a real customer came in, a distracted-looking woman in a yellow tracksuit carrying an umbrella. She dashed to the counter and threw down a package to be mailed and a five-dollar bill. Suzy's perma-grin was back as she rang up the bill and handed over change with a casualness that indicated the woman was a regular.

After the woman left, Suzy inserted a key into the copier's slot and pushed a small green button that read OVERRIDE. "Copy away."

"Sure you won't get in trouble for this?" asked Natalie, giving Suzy one last chance to back out, even though it seemed unlikely anyone could pressure the acerbic girl into anything she didn't want to do. Well, maybe her parents.

"Absolutely," said Suzy, pulling herself up onto the counter and sitting there with her legs dangling down. "No one will ever know. However, I do expect to be addressed as Madame Patron of the Arts from now on."

Natalie snorted as she changed some settings so the machine would turn her single-sided originals into a booklet. "How about next issue I put you in my list of thank-yous?"

"Fine."

Natalie plopped the originals into the automatic feeder and hit start. Out came three issues of her zine: twenty-four pages of trivia in the life of a teenage girl. They were slightly askew, so she adjusted the settings. The machine began to chug its way through 100 copies. She took the first copies over to the counter and folded them before passing them to Suzy. Ruth bounded over to check it out too.

"They need to be stapled, but I can do that at home. You know you're a serious zinester when you invest in a long-reach stapler. I call mine Stanley."

"This is so-o-o-o cool," said Ruth. "I should make a zine."

"I hate watching people flip through it in front of me, though," said Natalie, as Ruth and Suzy started to do just that. "Makes my skin crawl."

"But you sell this to complete strangers," said Suzy, mystified.

Natalie sighed. "True. For some reason, I'm compelled to share my personal life with the entire world, but only through the zine, not in person."

"You're weird," said Ruth, twirling a piece of hair around one finger.

"And that's why we like you," said Suzy, flipping her copy shut.

Ruth laughed and leaned over the counter to rest on her elbows. "So, now you have no choice but to tell us all about your visit to Jacob's."

"Well, there's not much to tell. I just hung out with him and his dad."

"What's their house like?"

"Normal, except that Isaac makes these tiny figurines, hundreds of little ceramic hand-painted things. They're really beautiful. He arranges them to form traditional folk tales and stories."

"Who knew our school janitor was a fine artist?" said Suzy.

"It *was* odd."

"What else did you talk about?" asked Ruth, bored by the figurines.

"Isaac really doesn't like Jefferson or Mr. Wojcik."

"Nobody does," said Suzy. "Except the guys on the football team. They're in love with him."

"Did you hear about his total meltdown last year, in the middle of a game?" asked Ruth. "According to Matt, he called the team off the field to discuss their next play. Someone questioned his decision, so he went ballistic. Completely lost it.

Jefferson had to come down from the bleachers and walk him off the field."

"Did they finish the game?" asked Natalie.

"Who cares," said Ruth, waving a hand. "Our team never makes the playoffs anyway. We're a collegiate. The tech schools cream us. My brother should have been born into a family that doesn't care about academics, then he would have gone to a sports-oriented high school and had a chance at a scholarship. At least, that's what he thinks."

Across the room, the photocopier stopped making noises. Natalie put the originals back in their protective sleeve and slipped them into her bag. For the next twenty minutes, the girls folded copies of the zine and gossiped. At nine-thirty on the dot, Suzy pulled out her math textbook and snapped, "Get out or look alive. Put those zines away. We're supposed to be studying."

Ruth, used to the routine, grabbed her binder and math book from her bag.

"Quickly," hissed Suzy at Natalie.

"I didn't bring my binder!" Natalie stuffed the folded zines into her bag, and took out her pirate notebook. She opened it randomly to a page with writing on it, and held her pen over top, as if she'd just finished writing a sentence.

The little cherubs above the door jingled. All three girls' heads turned simultaneously. A bright ball of energy swooshed into the room. Suzy's mother, Mrs. Moon, had tight auburn curls and piercing blue eyes. She wore pink canvas shoes, yellow leg warmers and a purple silk bomber jacket with a patterned silk scarf billowing out the top. A red plastic rain hat—the kind you

can buy at dollar stores—was tied tightly under her chin.

She passed the three girls without a glance and strode into a back room.

Mr. Moon, a good deal less flamboyant, trailed behind his wife. His short, bristly black hair was streaked with grey and he slouched forward into a sweater that was a little too big for him. He paused briefly to frown at his daughter, and asked a question in what sounded like Cantonese.

"Friends from school," replied Suzy.

He nodded at Ruth. "I already know Ruth. Hello, Ruth."

"How's business, Mr. Moon?"

"It's not the busiest time of year for an accountant, but I can't complain."

Ruth looked at Natalie. "Mr. Moon is my parents' accountant."

Natalie nodded, causing Mr. Moon's gaze to move on to her. He took in her hair and clothes. He looked at her notebook and frowned a second time. She quickly tilted it away from him, even though there was no way he could read the writing from so far away. He turned back to his daughter. "Who is this?"

"Natalie Fuentes. She's new at Western."

"New at Western?" he asked. "No one new goes to Western."

"I did," said Natalie, smiling her sweetest, most innocent smile. "But then, my dad and I are from out of town, so we didn't know about all the strange things happening there."

His eyebrows shot up. Just then, Mrs. Moon burst out of the back room pushing a baby stroller. Bundled up in a white fleece jacket and strapped into a kiddie seatbelt was a small blond terrier with pointy white ears and a long tongue. It was the same size as a toddler. The woman didn't pause, just whizzed straight out the door and took off down the rainy street. Mr. Moon disappeared into the back room without another word.

Natalie looked over at Suzy, hoping for an explanation other than "My mom's nuts."

Suzy sighed. "That's our dog, Jade. She got hit by a car and broke both her back legs, so she can't go outside on her own. Mother's convinced she still needs to be walked three times a day or she'll get depressed, so they go on power walks. Mom removes the diaper just long enough for Jade to do her business on our competitors' properties."

"I see," said Natalie. She glanced over at Ruth, but the blonde girl was skimming an article about Johnny Depp in *People* as though it was all normal.

"You probably want to be gone by the time she gets back," added Suzy.

"Right," said Ruth, jamming the magazine back into the rack. "Or she'll start quizzing us on our homework. That's what happened last time I overstayed my welcome, Natalie. Mrs. Moon wouldn't let me leave until I memorized everything we'd studied in math class that week."

"Welcome to my life," said Suzy, wincing at the memory. She glanced nervously at the door. "See you tomorrow at lunch?"

"Lunch," chorused the other two girls, escaping through the door just in time. Mrs. Moon barreled around a nearby corner, stroller flying in front of her, and charged into the store.

Later that night, Natalie was at her desk in her bedroom, doing the math homework she was supposed to be working on with Suzy, when she received an anonymous email. She clicked to open it and saw that it only contained two sentences.

To: zinegirl@freemail.com
From: 666@freemail.com
Subject: Warning

Watch your back! Western can be lethal for outsiders.

She stared at the screen for a couple of seconds, then sat back. It had to be from Ramiro because the email address contained half of his tag name, Ram666, and he was the only person she'd given her email to other than Ruth, Suzy and Jacob. But why would Ramiro feel the need to warn her anonymously? Was he threatening her? Was *he* the one who sprayed her locker?

She wrote back:

To: 666@freemail.com
From: zinegirl@freemail.com
Re: Warning

Is this a threat? I could really use some information here. What do you know?

For the rest of the evening, she checked her inbox obsessively, even fell asleep with the monitor on, but there was no answer. What she couldn't figure out was why Ramiro and his friends would have any motive to intimidate her.

chapter Seven

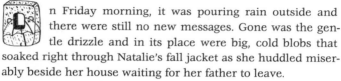

n Friday morning, it was pouring rain outside and there were still no new messages. Gone was the gentle drizzle and in its place were big, cold blobs that soaked right through Natalie's fall jacket as she huddled miserably beside her house waiting for her father to leave.

She consoled herself with the thought that today was the last day she would be forced to skip gym, provided things went according to plan between Matt and Missy at the dance that night. The thought wasn't much comfort when she shifted her soggy butt on the cold pavement and went over the emailed warning in her head. Not even putting The Shins' "Caring Is Creepy" in repeat mode on her MP3 player improved her mood.

By half-past nine, when her father still hadn't left, she started to wonder what was up. Every other day this week, he'd left at least twenty minutes earlier. She had to take off herself in fifteen minutes and didn't want him to catch her sneaking past the front window.

Then she heard the phone ring inside, and the rush of her father's footsteps as he hurried over to answer the living room extension.

"Hello, Brenda," said Jorge. His voice carried perfectly

through the window to Natalie's ears. "You're twenty minutes late. I see—a press conference... What did I expect? Well, she's fine, I guess... Having a few problems at her new school. She promised me she would call... She didn't? Well, she's been busy. We've both been busy. I don't know! We're trying to settle into our new lives here. I'll make sure she calls, or, at the very least, writes you another email.... Fine, suit yourself. I won't push her... Well, which is it, Brenda?"

Hands over her ears, Natalie scurried out of the alley, leaped on her wet bike and pushed the pedals with thoroughly soggy sneakers, trying to remember who wrote the book *All Families Are Psychotic*. Whoever the author was had a point. She didn't even bother to avoid the puddles. The weather matched her mood.

Thankfully, her school day was uneventful, and it had stopped raining and warmed up a little by the time Natalie and the Hamiltons set out for the dance. Suzy wasn't able to convince her parents to let her go. Unfortunately, Jorge thought a dance would be the perfect thing for Natalie. She tied a sweatshirt around her waist and willed herself to enjoy the evening. Dances weren't really her thing.

Matt walked a little ahead of the two girls. He was recounting in excruciating detail some squabble between coach Wojcik and a teammate during the afternoon's football practice. One of the defensive backs fumbled a play and got screamed at or something.

Natalie tuned him out. She had no interest in hearing what made the old coach, Marsden, a great role model for young jocks, or how Wojcik was a jerk. Matt's voice formed a soothing backdrop as her mind wandered to an email she'd received from her mother just before leaving the house.

Her mom was upset that Natalie hadn't called her in over a month. Natalie made a mental note to send her a present or something—maybe the new issue of *My Very Secret Life*. She could express a package and that way Natalie might get away with not having to speak to her on the phone... Learning about your daughter's life through a zine, instead of a conversation, had to be better than nothing.

"I hope Jacob's there," said Ruth, startling Natalie out of her private thoughts.

"Why?" asked Matt.

"Because he's cute, stupid."

Matt groaned. "Oh right, you have the hots for geekboy."

She slapped his arm playfully. "He's the only guy worth spending two minutes with in our entire school."

Matt coddled his forearm, mock-scowling. "Hey! Thanks a lot."

"No offence," said Ruth, but she didn't rescind her earlier comment.

They were approaching the school. At night, the building looked completely different. More imposing and a little eerie, because all the lights in the classroom windows were out. Floods lit the front entrance. All the other doors were locked, so kids were forced to go in that way, past two teachers who were searching for illegal substances.

It appeared the dance was already in full swing, though they hadn't even made it inside yet. Half a dozen teens lounged on the grass out front, staring up at the dark sky. A couple cuddled behind some bushes. Four boys down near the street who were drinking beer drew Natalie's attention with loud laughter. She noticed Ramiro was one of them. He lounged against a car and watched her head over. The Hamiltons went on ahead.

"Not exactly your scene, is it?" she asked.

Ramiro scratched his chest lazily. "And what is my scene, Maggie? I'd like to hear your opinion on this, seeing as you've known me exactly three days."

"A dark alley," she retorted. "Filled with blank brick canvases."

"I admit I don't avoid the dark alleys. Thought I'd try out a high school dance tonight, to remind myself how much I hate them."

She leaned next to him and waved to the Hamiltons, who were hovering near the door, waiting for her. Ruth glanced meaningfully at Ramiro, shrugged and disappeared inside.

Natalie turned back to Ramiro. She knew he'd seen Ruth's warning look and was relieved when he didn't comment, but instead focused on someone coming up behind her.

"Jake, my man, you always leave me waiting."

Jacob was grinning guiltily.

"You came too?" she asked, surprised.

"Sure," he said, jamming his hands deep into his jeans pockets.

"How's your dad doing?"

His eyes glazed over. Clearly, he didn't want to talk about his father tonight. She kicked herself and said the first thing that came to mind. "Um, I think Ruth's looking for you."

"Who?"

"My friend Ruth Hamilton."

"Oh, right."

"She said something about trying to find you inside."

"My dad likes you," he said out of the blue, dancing around the truth she'd left unspoken—that Ruth liked him.

Next to her, Ramiro whistled long and low. "Maggie already met your dad?"

"She came over for dinner," said Jacob, then quickly added, "to talk about the attack."

Ramiro's eyes sparked. "Sure. How's the old man doing?"

Jacob rammed his hands into his hip pockets. "Better than a few days ago."

"That's good. I'd hate to see anything bad happen to that guy. He's always been nice to me."

"He thinks you're a great artist."

Natalie kept silent. She was picturing Isaac in the kitchen, dropping the dinner plate. She could see Jacob's hands clench into fists in his pockets.

"I brought the latest issue of my zine," she blurted out, hoping to change the topic of conversation once again. She slipped off her canvas bag and extracted two copies of *My Very Secret Life*. Jacob's face brightened. His fists unclenched and he reached for one. Ramiro also accepted a copy, curiosity splashed across his face.

"Don't read it now, okay? I'm weird about people reading it in front of me. But I do expect email feedback. You both have my address."

Jacob slipped it in his back pocket. Ramiro looked a little caught off guard by the email comment. He walked over to the nearby car and threw the zine onto the passenger seat through an open window, then paused to say something to his friends.

"Well, I think I'll head inside to see what's going on," said Jacob.

"Have fun."

He walked off just as Ramiro came back over.

"So, I got your message yesterday," she said.

He looked perturbed. "How'd you know it was me?"

"I'm not an idiot. Your email address is part of your tag name."

"And Jacob showed you my tag. That bastard." He licked his lips and took a deep breath. "Look, Maggie, I just wanted to warn you. I overheard those blonde girls talking and there's no love lost between me and them. Understand?"

"You mean Missy and company?"

He nodded once. "They know something."

"About the attack?"

He scrunched up his face. "I think so."

"What did you hear them say?"

"I caught the end of a sentence about how Isaac had it coming to him."

She sat down on the grass and leaned back against a lamp post. "Maybe they're behind it all—the attacks, the thefts... It would be just like that movie about the bank-robbing cheerleaders."

After a moment, Ramiro took a seat beside her. "Truth is," he said, "if I didn't see the attacker was a man, I might think it was one of them. But I do have some other theories about who the thief might be."

Natalie jolted upright. "Who?"

His eyes flicked over to his buddies. A minute ago, they'd

been jostling around. Now they were quiet. Listening to the conversation? "I don't squeal," growled Ramiro.

"Not even if it might save Jacob's dad's life?"

Ramiro ripped up a few blades of grass with muscular brown fingers. "Look, I can't talk about it."

"Seems unlikely that two people are sabotaging Western High."

His head drooped forward. She couldn't see his face from that angle.

She forced herself to think about something else. Different noises floated out from inside: laughter, dance music and the occasional drunken screech. Some of Ramiro's friends started wrestling on the lawn. The empty beer bottles at their feet made her realize her bladder was full. She peered at the entrance, which was guarded by two teachers.

"Wonder if the bathrooms are crazy."

"Of course they are," said Ramiro. "Think of all the girls who need to check their makeup and puke in the stalls."

"Right." She stood up and made her way to the doors. Through them, she could see a bunch of unfamiliar kids.

Natalie screwed up her nerve and pushed inside. She passed several clusters of friends, and a couple making out in the lobby. The boy had crazy braces and it looked like he was trying to inhale his girlfriend's face.

She rounded a corner and pushed into the gymnasium. It was pretty dark. The only light came from some whirling spots mounted on the bleachers and a huge disco ball shooting off rainbow-colored triangles. She made her way to the change rooms, which were being used as bathrooms, and almost plowed into

Matt Hamilton, who looked pretty cozy, leaning into a blonde girl—Missy. Her back was against the wall. His face was flushed and he was whispering something into her ear.

Natalie tried to make herself inconspicuous as she passed them, but Matt's eyes swung around at the last second. He wiggled his eyebrows over Missy's shoulder. Had he been drinking for the past half hour? It was none of Natalie's business. She assumed he was thanking her for setting him up with Missy, so she smiled encouragingly. The blonde girl's face tipped toward her and it wasn't scowling.

So far, so good, thought Natalie. She continued down the hall. A little farther along, Lynette was standing all by herself, arms crossed as she leaned against the wall. She looked bored. Natalie caught her eye and the girl, having witnessed the exchange with Matt, gave an unenthusiastic finger wave. A lack of enthusiasm, Natalie could handle. It was a million times better than outright hatred.

She got in line outside the bathroom and waited her turn. When she finally made it into a stall, it was disgusting. There were ashes on the floor, and it seemed like the last twenty girls hadn't hit the bowl.

She washed her hands and wandered around the gym for a while, trying to find Ruth and Jacob. They were nowhere. A sickly romantic R&B song came on and she headed back outside, relieved to get out of the human crush. Ramiro was still where she'd left him, sitting against the lamp post, only now he was nursing a beer.

Natalie sat down next to him, relaxed, and pulled out her notebook to write for a while. At some point, she looked up and

realized she was ready to head home. She yawned exaggerat-edly. "What time is it?"

"Time for you to count some sheep."

"Seriously," she insisted, putting the notebook away and checking her various pockets for her cell phone. She turned it on. Ten-thirty. "Damn. I've gotta go."

"My buddy Eddie'll drive you."

"Which one's Eddie?" She followed his gaze. "The one with the car?"

Ramiro nodded. Eddie was a lean, muscular guy lounging in the driver's seat of the ancient Mazda, with one brown arm poking out of the tinted window as he rested a half-empty beer on the ledge. He reached out and none too gently punched the leg of a buddy who was perched on the hood. The guy slid off the car, laughing like a hyena. Apparently, it was a routine: sit on the car, get kicked off, etc. Natalie had a momentary urge to ask about the tattoo on his arm—it looked like a sideways egg from her position. Then Eddie took a healthy gulp from his beer and she decided now was not the time.

"Thanks, but I'll walk. I'm not a huge fan of drunk drivers and it's only, like, six blocks."

Ramiro gave her an odd look but his eyes were warm. "Let me walk you, then."

Would she be safer with or without him? she wondered. "Thanks, but I'm fine."

"Suit yourself, Maggie," Ramiro said dryly, lifting one hand in a cool wave.

She headed down the path to the sidewalk and set off at a brisk clip. Belatedly, she realized she hadn't said goodbye to

either of the Hamiltons. It took some getting used to, making friends this quickly. This wasn't normal behavior for her.

The streets were relatively empty, but she'd learned at a young age how to maneuver a new city at night. She kept her head up, made eye contact with anyone who passed her, and acted like she'd fight back if anyone tried to mug her. Toronto wasn't New York, so she probably didn't have to worry about getting mugged for the eight dollars and thirty cents in her pocket, but still...

Stretches of sidewalk shone with reflected light from unadorned street lamps. The lamps fit with this city, she decided, comparing it in her mind to the cultured chaos of Buenos Aires and the self-importance of New York. Toronto wasn't beautiful, but it seemed to work. Had its own rhythm.

When she heard girls tittering behind her, she thought nothing of it. They must have left the dance just after she did. But their voices got louder and it sounded like they were catching up to her, so she casually turned to get a look. The flock of skinny girls in tight jeans and brightly colored shirts bumped against one another as they walked, as if they'd had one too many vodka coolers. Two girls at the front whispered something when they saw her staring.

Natalie picked up speed. She definitely didn't want to be surrounded by the drunk and fabulous. She clipped along for a block. The wind carried wild laughter to her ears. They reminded her of hyenas. Her heart jumped into her throat when she heard a screech. Then someone yelled, "You better run, bitch."

She spared the briefest glance behind her. The girls were

now running as quickly as their Barbie pumps and sequined flip-flops could carry them. She caught a flash of straight blonde hair and recognized Sandy Blatchford. Her pretty face was distorted. She looked tanked.

Natalie started to run, cursing under her breath. She thought she'd dealt with the Golden Girls. Maybe Ruth was right and the only way to get them to leave her alone was direct confrontation.

Footsteps rang in her ears. Her lungs started to burn, but she couldn't afford to look back and risk losing more ground. She had no idea how far behind her they were.

"You're so dead!" one of them yelled. Natalie thought it might have been Sandy.

She pushed herself to go faster. Only two blocks to go. She couldn't believe she'd refused Ramiro's offer to walk her home. Casting around desperately for a convenience store, her usual fall-back plan for scary situations, she saw nothing was open.

"Hey, bitch, we're gonna get you!" screeched the same voice, and Natalie knew beyond a doubt that it was Sandy. She was the puppet-master tonight.

Desperately, Natalie shoved her hand into her bag, slowing down a little as she groped for her cell phone. She pushed a couple of buttons and autodialed home. It rang once, twice, three times. The answering machine came on. She dropped the phone into her bag. Where was her father?

The girls were right behind her now, feet slapping the pavement loudly, breath loud enough to hear. Then a car squealed up onto the sidewalk right in front of her, making her jump. The doors opened.

"Hey, Maggie," said a male voice—Ramiro.

She stopped running and pressed her hand into a stitch in her side. Breathing in ragged gasps, she watched Ramiro and Eddie get out of the car, arms crossed menacingly. Eddie's tattooed bicep was clearly visible. They looked fierce.

Sandy and her gang of girls were actually backing up at that point. Natalie felt sick as she padded over to the car, keeping a wary eye on the girls. Up close, she could see not one of them would be scary on her own. But together they were a mob. It wouldn't have been a fair fight.

"What's your problem?" she spat at Sandy.

The blonde girl tossed her hair. Unlike the other girls, she didn't look frightened of the boys—she was still furious. "Back off, or you're going to get hurt. I swear ..."

"What have I ever done to you?"

"You've been poking around in other people's business ever since you got here."

Eddie walked up and got in Sandy's face, chest puffed out. "If you touch a hair on her head, you'll answer to us."

"Oooh, the fallen angel's gonna beat me up?"

"Consider this your only warning," growled Eddie. "Now, go curl each other's eyelashes or whatever it is you do in your free time."

Sandy's eyes were narrowed to slits. She was seething, but she backed away and forced a final laugh before strutting off with her gang.

Natalie felt Ramiro's calming hand rest on her arm.

Eddie shook his head. "Unbelievable. Pulls this act like she's the queen of Western and we're all her peasants."

Ramiro snorted. "That puff of a girl and her blonde friends have scared more new kids away than anything else that's been happening at our school."

"She's definitely intimidating," agreed Natalie.

"Don't let her get to you."

"Especially when she's got six friends with her," added Eddie. "Let's head."

He walked around his car. Natalie hesitated, though to be honest, for a guy who'd been guzzling beer ten minutes ago, he was acting surprisingly sober.

Ramiro noticed her hesitation and chuckled. "Damn. She thinks you're drunk, man."

"What the—" Eddie looked confused for a moment, then reached through the car window and pulled out a half-empty bottle. "Because of my Not Beer?"

"That's de-alcoholized?" asked Natalie, feeling incredibly stupid.

"Maggie," said Ramiro, "you're so convinced we're a bunch of thugs that I didn't want to burst your bubble. Eddie's a responsible guy."

She looked sheepish.

"I'm bagged," said Eddie, yawning. "Let's head. Either get in the car or start walking so we can follow you home and make sure you arrive safely."

"I'll take a lift," she said quickly, opening the back door and pushing aside a stack of black and white graffiti stickers to slip into the seat.

Ramiro and Eddie got in the front.

"Why'd she call you a fallen angel?" Natalie asked Eddie.

"She wants my body," he joked, deliberately avoiding the question.

Somehow he already knew where she lived, because he didn't ask for directions, just turned down the right street and pulled up in front of her house.

"Eddie was Western's star quarterback last year," said Ramiro, as she was getting out.

She paused by the driver's window and bent down. "I thought Matt Hamilton was the quarterback."

Eddie let out a dismissive breath. "That guy's nuthin' next to me."

"Humble much?" joked Natalie. "He's M.V.P."

"Not yet, he's not. The season's just started." Eddie bent low to glare at the house next to Natalie's.

"Why should my man be humble?" shot Ramiro. "He's right. Matt Hamilton doesn't deserve the title. Everyone knows Eddie would have been M.V.P. again if it weren't for that racist coach kicking him off the team and getting him expelled. Eddie's sick on the field."

"Mr. Wojcik hates Eddie?" asked Natalie, trying to keep up.

Eddie leaned out the window and spat on the street. "Let's just say my football career hit a brick wall thanks to him."

"Not just football," said Ramiro. "Your academic career too."

"Burned me bad," said Eddie, grimacing. "But that's a sob story for another time. You're home. Go. I want to watch you lock the door behind you."

Natalie ran up her steps, a little irritated by his commanding tone, but happy to be home. Lights flickered in the living room window, indicating her dad was watching television. She

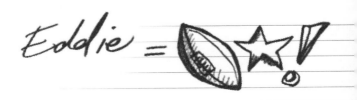

unlocked the door and heard the *M.A.S.H.* theme song. Her father's favorite show. The door locked behind her with a click and the TV's sound died.

"Nati?"

"Yeah, it's me. Didn't you hear the phone ring just now?"

"I think maybe I left the cordless upstairs." She heard him getting up from the couch. She shuffled up a couple of steps, knowing he wouldn't let her escape to her room without a brief greeting. Sure enough, he appeared in the hall, rubbing his eyes sleepily. She leaned over and air-kissed next to his cheek. "Did you call?"

"Yeah, but it's nothing," she lied. "I'm exhausted. Need sleep."

He straightened up, remembering something. "I received a phone call from your school saying you weren't in gym class today. What's going on?"

Damn. She'd forgotten to erase the message before leaving for the dance. At least he only knew about today, not the entire week. "I... wasn't feeling well."

"Why not? Are you ill?"

"No, uh, it's that time of the month."

"Oh. Well, I thought maybe something terrible happened." He put his head in his hands and groaned dramatically. "*Dios mío*, just give me one single day without getting a call from the police or your principal!"

"Don't worry, Dad. Everything's fine," she heard herself saying, though inside everything felt wrong. The last thing she wanted to do was worry him. He'd keep her in the house for the rest of her life. "I'll be back in gym on Monday. I'm just super tired right now."

"We'll talk tomorrow," he said, and she heard determination in his voice.

She dragged herself up to her bedroom, pulled the door shut and lay down. If it weren't for Ramiro and Eddie, she'd have been in big trouble out there. She still didn't totally trust them, but was lucky they showed up when they did. Sandy was out for blood. Why?

Pretty much all the people she'd met since her first day at Western could be categorized as "suspicious." Isaac had managed to piss off his boss—Jefferson—and her boss—the school-board superintendent—with that anal equipment-tracking database. Ramiro and his buds definitely knew more than they let on. Jacob's been arrested for hacking, the blondes keep telling her to butt out, and Wojcik the football coach was apparently not a very nice man.

It seemed unlikely that Ruth and Suzy were involved in any way, but still, the only people she could definitely trust were her parents, and now they were on opposite sides of the world. It felt like her mother had sloughed her off. Sure, her mom made an attempt to keep in touch, but she was so far away. It took some getting used to, having only a dad around to talk to now, no mother. As she waited for sleep to envelop her, Natalie had never felt more alone.

The next morning, her father was already drinking coffee and eating a slice of egg pie he called *tortilla* when she came downstairs. There was an empty plate waiting for her across the counter. He poured himself another cup of coffee and took a sip while she served herself. It was so obviously time for The Big Talk.

Natalie automatically cast around for some way to cut him off at the pass. "So I was thinking of heading to the mall. I might pick up something for Mom. You know what they say... absence making the heart grow stronger or something."

He put down his mug. "Good idea."

She was really going to look at watches and see if she could identify the one the attacker had been wearing, but cleverly neglected to mention this. Instead, she took a deep breath and pressed forward, laying it on thick. "It's weird that she's so far away from us. I mean, it was always us against the world. No matter how bad 'us' got."

He buried his face in his coffee mug, clearly not sure how to respond.

"All the bad times are there in my head, crowding out the good memories, but I miss her."

"I have to admit that's a relief to hear," said her dad, rousing himself from his coffee. "A girl needs her mother. I've been worried about you—the stress of the divorce, the move, getting used to a new school..."

"Dad, I've managed to take care of myself in war zones all over the world. This is Toronto. It's relatively safe."

"I'm just concerned, Nati." He sighed. "But I suppose a visit to a Mecca of Greed is about as safe as you can get in this country."

She burst out laughing. "By Mecca of Greed, you're referring to the mall?"

He nodded. "Sure. I'll give you some money, just make sure the present isn't garbage."

She rolled her eyes. "Like I would get her something bad! Thanks a lot. A book, dad. I was planning to get her a book."

"Mecca of Greed"
(good one dad 😊)

chapter eight

 atalie looked left and right when she exited her house, but no skinny girls were lurking behind any of the trees, waiting to jump her.

The only person in sight was Ruth Hamilton, and she was huddled on her front steps, listening to headphones. Her golden curls bounced perkily, making the miserable expression on her face seem even more grim in comparison. When she noticed Natalie, she jumped up and ran over. "Did your dad tell you I came by twice already?"

"No," said Natalie. "I guess he was distracted. He thinks I've lost it."

"Huh." Ruth shifted from one foot to the other anxiously. "What happened to you last night?"

"Left early. Got chased down the street by a mob of angry girls."

Ruth looked shocked.

"It's true. My walk home was the most exciting part of my night." She told Ruth about the Barbie Gang, and how Ramiro and Eddie showed up just in time to save her ass.

"What were they going to do?"

"Beat me up."

"No way! It's a good thing those guys followed you."

"I'll say." Natalie bent to unlock her bike.

"Going anywhere fun?"

"The mall," said Natalie. "To see if I can identify the watch the attacker was wearing."

"*Please* take me with you," Ruth begged. "My mom's on a total rampage. She tried to wake me in time for dance class this morning, but I fell back asleep, and now she's out for blood. She's like a werewolf on the full moon."

Natalie stifled a grin as she tried to reconcile that image with the one her father'd painted of Mrs. Hamilton as jam maker and welcoming neighbor. "What time was it?"

"Seven-thirty!"

Natalie shuddered. "What did she expect? You got home late last night."

Ruth nodded and shot a glare at her house. "I'm dying here, all because my brother and La Missy were fused at the hip. Not that you'd know. You hung out with those thugs all night."

"Matt and Missy were making out in the gym when I went to the bathroom."

"It got worse. Much worse. By the end of the night, I had to pull them off each other. And now they're in love. He's taking her to Red Lobster."

"Guess it's serious if he's taking her to Red Lobster," quipped Natalie.

"Apparently Missy *lo-o-oves* shrimp," said Ruth, grimacing. "Anyway, can I tag along to the mall? If I don't get away from here, my mother will make me practice in our basement studio until my feet bleed."

"Sure, grab your bike. You can show me the best way to get there."

Ruth clapped her hands excitedly and ran off to get her bike.

As they rode through a maze of side streets toward downtown, Natalie found herself asking, "So how did it go with you and Jacob?"

She really didn't want to find out they were a couple now too. They weren't suited for each other at all. Besides, when Natalie was over at his house, she'd felt some kind of connection. She didn't think she'd imagined it.

"We sat around and I pretended to be interested in the Internet all night," said Ruth, clearly miffed. "Jacob blabbed on and on about computers. Didn't make a single move. I mean nothing. Not even the yawn and stretch to put his arm around my shoulder when we were sitting on a bench behind the school. Zero. I'm starting to think Matt's right about him."

"He's been through a lot lately, maybe he just doesn't want to rush into anything."

"Maybe," said Ruth, but doubt crept into her voice.

"You think he's interested?"

"I don't know," she said. "It's really hard to tell with that guy."

The girls headed off. To get to the mall, they crossed through Chinatown—Natalie definitely wanted to visit the hectic neighborhood again later—and rode along trendy Queen Street West, where the cars were so thick, they were forced to ride single-file. Conversation became impossible.

They locked their bikes to a shaky, overloaded stand that would be nirvana for a bike thief, and went inside the mall. Teenagers swarmed through clothing stores and loitered on every bench, killing time and people-watching.

When they passed a group of guys wearing baggy clothes and baseball caps sitting near a tall fountain, one of them leaned over to ogle Ruth's legs under her flouncing mini-skort— half-skirt, half-shorts—and muttered something at a friend. He stood up to intercept them.

Ruth didn't notice: her eyes frantically bounced from one clothing shop to the next. Natalie made a rude gesture and mouthed the words "Dream on" at the guy behind her back. He did an about-face and went back to scouting out an easy conquest.

"It's weird," said Natalie, interrupting Ruth's shopping-inspired daydreams. "I always think I'll enjoy being at the mall until I actually get here."

"Wha—" mumbled Ruth. She was like a moth drawn to a light bulb as she wandered over to a display of scoop-neck tops in every color imaginable.

"Nothing." They passed a bookstore and Natalie tugged on Ruth's arm to break her trance. "Let's go in here. I'm going to pick out something for my mom."

"Yawn," said Ruth, eyes on a rack of low-cut jeans nearby. "Isn't she a writer? She's probably already got a million."

"Yes, but she's on location, so it's all dry, researchy stuff. I'm going to get her Isabel Allende's new novel."

"Who's she?"

"An exiled Chilean. My mom's favorite author."

It took Natalie very little time to locate the book on a best-seller pile at the front of the store and pick out a birthday card in the stationery section. It took more time to track down Ruth in the magazine section and then pay.

They wandered on and found a watch store with a big men's section. Natalie peered in the window.

"The one Isaac Kaufman's attacker wore was kind of dressy—silver and gold with some kind of orange logo in the middle. Might have been a sports team."

"My brother wants a Raiders watch that sounds just like that," said Ruth. "But their logo's black."

"The football team?"

"Yeah. He's hoping he'll get it as a present from the school when he's named M.V.P. at the end of the season."

"Do they give out watches every year?"

"As far as I know they do it for all the teams, not just football."

So that meant at least a dozen current students owned one, including Eddie.

Together they searched through the racks of men's watches, until Natalie found one that looked very similar to the one she'd seen. It had alternating silver- and gold-plated links and a silver face with a blue Toronto Blue Jays logo behind the hands.

Natalie asked a hovering salesman if he had similar models with red logos on them, but he didn't have any in stock. "How about a catalogue?" she asked.

The guy shook his head and wandered away in a huff, having determined she wouldn't be purchasing anything today.

They retraced their steps to their bikes and headed home. Once they were out of the craziest traffic, Natalie called up to Ruth: "What do you know about Eddie Chango?"

"Why, do you like him?" teased Ruth, slanting a sly look back at Natalie, who was riding behind her.

"I'm just curious."

"Well, he's a great football player. Maybe the best Western ever had. They say he attacked Mr. Wojcik. Just, bam!—lost it for no reason. That's why he was expelled."

"For no reason?"

Ruth shrugged. "He's got a reputation. I don't know the specifics. You should ask Matt."

"Think he'd be home now?"

"Should be. Unless he managed to escape my parents too. Or Missy the Witch got her claws in him."

The two girls rode home and dropped their bikes on the Hamiltons' front lawn. Ruth ran inside to get her brother while Natalie waited on the steps. She came back outside a couple of minutes later, tugging on her brother's arm, and pulled the door shut behind her. Matt was wearing too-short track pants and an old team shirt—not the kind of clothes a big man on campus would ordinarily be caught dead wearing.

"Hurry. Natalie needs to talk to you," Ruth was saying.

Matt looked annoyed. "I was studying. If I don't keep up a C average, I'll be kicked off the team and it'll be *your* fault. Besides, Mom's looking for you. Don't you have to go practice your routine?"

"Shh." Ruth glanced nervously at the closed front door. "Don't tell her I'm here."

Matt rolled his eyes and turned to Natalie, waiting for her to explain why he was outside. She noticed he was still carrying a cordless phone. It seemed more likely he'd been blabbing on the phone with Missy when Ruth grabbed him, not studying at all.

"Ruth told me there's a Raiders watch..." started Natalie.

Ruth interrupted impatiently: "She thinks the guy who attacked Isaac Kaufman was wearing one of those NFL watches they give the team's MVP every year."

Matt frowned.

"Do you know anyone who has one with a red logo on it?" asked Natalie.

"Sure. Eddie Chango. Coach Marsden gave him his favorite team, the Buccaneers."

"What does it look like?"

He put his hand on the doorknob. "I have a magazine upstairs. I can show you a picture."

"Great."

He disappeared inside, came back carrying a rolled-up magazine moments later, and opened it to a dog-eared page. There were dozens of watches like the one in the store. Each had a different team's logo on the face behind the golden hands. Natalie located the Buccaneers watch. The logo was a little red pirate flag. She thought it might be a bit darker than the one on the attacker's wrist, closer to the Browns' logo, a reddish-orange helmet. But she couldn't be sure. She'd only caught a quick glimpse.

"When did Wojcik become the football coach?" she asked, thinking how ironic it was that the only thing that could get her worked up about football was a possible link to the mystery.

Matt made a dismissive sound and leaned against the porch railing. "End of last year. It was Marsden for twenty years, until he retired in December."

"I didn't realize it was that recent."

"I've been kind of hoping Marsden will miraculously reappear on the field one day and pick up where he left off." Matt glanced away, as if he was uncomfortable admitting it. "It's just that he was the nicest man you'd ever meet. He knew how to get the best from us. Wojcik's coaching style is more aggressive. Some guys love him. I guess that's how it is—you either love him or hate him."

"Do you think Wojcik's coaching style affected Eddie's ability to play on the team?"

Matt's leg started to swing back and forth. "Absolutely. It was always a fight for Eddie, once Marsden retired. Wojcik was constantly putting him down, making him do extra laps, that kind of thing. And Eddie has a short fuse. Doesn't put up with much. Bit of a loose cannon."

"What did the team do when Wojcik started treating him badly?"

Matt looked guilty. "Not much. I mean, at first we thought it was just Wojcik's coaching style. But then it became clear he had a hate on for Eddie and that if anyone didn't like it, they'd be sitting on the sidelines permanently."

"Do you believe what people say about Eddie attacking Wojcik?"

"I have no idea what happened, because it went down in the locker room. But I remember earlier that day at practice, when Wojcik called him lazy one too many times. We thought Eddie was going to punch him, totally start whaling on him, but he just got in Wojcik's face, told him to back off and stalked away."

"Did anyone tell Jefferson what happened on the field?"

"Doubt it."

"Why not?"

"She's a woman," he admitted, after a moment.

"Typical!" chirped in Ruth.

"She wouldn't understand the kind of pressure put on the football team—even Marsden liked to pull the wool over her eyes."

"You know Eddie was expelled because of whatever happened that day?"

Matt looked confused. "Wojcik said it was due to aggressive behavior. Something must have happened. Something big."

The front door opened. A petite woman in her early forties with frosted blonde hair stuck her head out. "Ruthie, is that you?"

Ruth swore under her breath. "Yeah."

"I've been looking for you all morning! Where did you get off to?"

"I went to the mall with Natalie—Mom, this is Natalie Fuentes. She lives next door."

"Right," said the woman, extending a hand covered in flour. "Hello, Natalie. I met your father the other day. What a lovely man."

"Yes, he is," said Natalie, shaking the hand. It was limp.

Ruth groaned. "Mom, you call everyone lovely."

Her mother hitched up a warning eyebrow. "Shouldn't you be practicing, instead of prancing around town?"

Ruth's lower lip stuck out. She was sulking. "Whatever. Natalie was just leaving, anyhow."

"Well, then, goodbye, Natalie," said Mrs. Hamilton pointedly.

Natalie said a quick goodbye and headed to her house. As she entered, she yelled hello to her father, who was down in the basement setting up his darkroom. He'd probably be at it all weekend. Then she went upstairs to put the book in a padded envelope with the latest issue of her zine and a few photos of the house. She found her mother's most recent email message and transcribed the address of the hotel onto the package.

Satisfied she'd done her daughterly duty, she played Tetris while she sat there thinking about the watch dilemma. If she emailed Ramiro, she might be able to get Eddie's number and arrange a face-to-face meeting, so she could actually examine his wrist. But that would mean he'd have to be wearing it, which he might not be eager to do these days. Maybe she could figure out a way to get invited to his house and poke around in his bedroom. Although, if he caught her, none of the graffiti boys would trust her again.

Now, more than ever, she was desperate to get a look at the student records in Jefferson's locked filing cabinet. She was pretty sure Eddie's folder would explain more about the incident that led to his expulsion than any second-hand gossip.

She opened her web browser and loaded up Jacob's website. She remembered seeing a link to his email address on the

About page. She clicked on it and sent him a quick note: "Do you have keys for the entire school?"

It might take him a little while to respond, she knew, even if he was sitting at his computer, so she brought the package for her mom down to the foyer for her dad to courier and made herself a sandwich, which she carried back upstairs to munch in her room.

A response from Jacob was already sitting in her inbox: "Not over email. Let's talk in person."

She wrote: "This afternoon?"

He sent an answer immediately: "Come over in an hour."

"Okay, see you soon," she typed back.

She finished off her sandwich and traipsed down to the basement so she could spend a few minutes with her dad. The easiest way to convince him to let her go out again was to tell him the truth: that she was going to hang out with her new friend, Jacob Kaufman. They might go to a local coffee shop or something to chat, because he was a little bummed about his dad's slow recovery.

Her father spared her a suspicious glance, but didn't ask any questions. Some prints were waiting in the developing tank, so he had to get to it before they became overexposed.

She biked over to Jacob's and found him waiting outside.

"Lock up your bike. Let's walk somewhere," he said.

"When I was riding to the mall this morning, I noticed that Coffee Lovers has a two-dollar special on iced moccachinos today. We could head there."

"Sounds great."

When they were a short distance from his house, Jacob

asked her why she wanted to know about the school keys. Natalie explained about being chased after the party, the watch she remembered the attacker wearing, and how she thought it was all somehow connected to Eddie being expelled. She finished by telling him about the locked filing cabinet in Jefferson's office, leaning close to whisper: "I need to see what's in that cabinet."

He pulled away. "You're asking me to help you break into our principal's confidential records?"

"That's one way to put it."

"Is there any other way?" he asked stiffly.

She wracked her brain for some less malevolent-sounding twist and came up empty. "I guess not. Look, I need your help. I think those files might help us figure out who's been doing these awful things to your father. There are answers in there, I just know."

"You *know*?" he asked, sarcastically.

She squeezed her hands together. "At this point, I'm out of other ideas. Do you have any?"

He thought about it. "Not exactly."

They arrived at Coffee Lovers and went inside to order their moccachinos. While they waited, Natalie kept sneaking sideways glances at Jacob. He was deep in thought, brow furrowed. She bit her lip, realizing she was putting a lot of faith in a boy she barely knew. He could turn her in to Jefferson and she'd get kicked out of school, just like Eddie.

They got their drinks and chose a table a little apart from the rest of the patrons. Jacob avoided her eyes. He scooped mouthfuls of whipped cream off the top of his drink. When he

finally looked up, there was a small dab of white cream on his upper lip. She fought an urge to reach over and wipe it off. A short burst of anxious laughter popped out.

"Natalie, this isn't funny," said Jacob. "Do you know how much trouble we could get in?"

She made her face stop grinning.

"You're determined to do this, with or without me?"

She nodded, hoping she could relieve any feelings of guilt on his part. The truth was she had no idea how she'd manage to get in there without a partner in crime.

He took another sip. "Fine. It just so happens my dad keeps a master set of keys for the entire school in his office."

She released a huge breath she hadn't realized she was holding. "I was hoping you might say something like that."

"Basically, you're using me for my keys?"

She laughed. "That's right."

"Figures."

How to respond? Fortunately, he didn't wait for her to come up with a sassy comeback.

"When do you plan on doing this?" he asked.

"Tonight."

He spat out a mouthful of coffee, hastily mopped it up with a napkin.

"It's a Saturday," she said. "The building will be empty."

"Not necessarily. There'll be at least one caretaker watching it, and sometimes the teachers with no lives come in on weekends to catch up on marking or prepare lessons."

"Almost empty, then. You have to admit, it's the quietest time of the week."

She could practically see gears turning in his head.

"True. But we'll need some supplies."

"I've already got one." She pulled out her penlight keychain and shone it in his eyes.

He blinked. "You, my dear Watson, are an amateur when it comes to gear. Let's go back to my place and plan this covert op."

"Only if you admit I'm the Sherlock in this partnership," she joked.

"You're more like Nancy Drew," he shot back.

"Then who does that make you, Joe Hardy?"

The corners of his mouth lifted. "Try Ned Nickerson."

"You wish."

"Maybe I do."

Natalie quickly decided that, once again, saying nothing was her best option.

They left Coffee Lovers and walked side by side, sipping what remained of their drinks. The hair on his arm brushed against hers. It was distracting. They were supposed to be planning a felony here, not flirting.

chapter nine

ack at his house, he brought her up to his room and opened a closet door she hadn't noticed last time. That's because it was covered with a huge map showing Internet connectivity across the world at midnight on December 31, 1999. She felt a thrill. This was his real base of operations. His secret gear room.

Jacob pulled assorted items out of the closet: a small but industrial-strength flashlight, two long-sleeved shirts (one of which he passed to her, indicating she should put it on), a pair of shiny purple toy radios and a backpack. He grabbed a mini crowbar. "Might not need this, but it's light, and incredibly strong."

"Where'd you get all this stuff?"

"This isn't the first time I've gone somewhere I'm not supposed to, Natalie. Though usually the buildings I enter are abandoned."

"What are you talking about?"

"I've done a little urban exploration." He tossed her a book called *Access All Areas*. "Ever heard of Ninjalicious?"

"Doesn't he make a zine?"

"He did. *Infiltration*. Died not too long ago, sadly. The last

thing he wrote was this bible. I've already read the section on entering active buildings. It's no big deal. Take a look."

The last item he collected was on his desk: a small rectangular case that looked like a jack-knife. He handed it to her. She prised open the case's cover and found a folded set of six lock picks, like bizarre dentist's tools, and a tiny instruction manual. She examined each of the picks. There was even a mini torque wrench that slid out of a slot at the end, where a toothpick or pair of tweezers sat in normal pocket knives.

"I got it on eBay for fifteen bucks," said Jacob. "It's a starter set."

"Who the hell would sell lock picks on eBay?"

"You wouldn't believe the stuff people sell on there. Cars. Jennifer Aniston's underwear..."

"You're like my own private Q!"

"It's Fuentes, Natalie Fuentes," he said, mugging James Bond.

She laughed. "You only live twice!" She folded up the picks and tucked the little case into his bag. "Please tell me what the toy radios are for."

"Constant communication. They might look like toys, but they work great, specially when you plug in earphones. That way they don't make any noise."

Jacob sat down at his computer and casually plucked at a few keys. She wondered again what she was getting herself into. He seemed to have a concept of right and wrong that didn't correspond very closely to the law. In fact, it was closer to the moral code of a graffiti artist. No wonder he got along so well with Ramiro.

"I should probably call my dad," she said after a while.

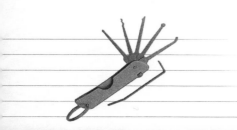

"Tell him we're going to a movie." He opened a browser and clicked over to the movie listings. "The local rep cinema's playing... *Baraka*. Surprise! They're always playing *Baraka*."

Jorge didn't answer, fortunately, so she left a message. "That was easy. He's probably still in his darkroom."

Jacob stuffed everything in his pack and checked his email one last time. "I'm starving." He glanced at the clock on his monitor. "It's dinnertime. My dad said he was going to order pizza. I'm sure there'll be enough for you."

"So he's feeling better?" she whispered on the stairs going down.

Jacob looked glum for the first time that afternoon. "Yeah, I just have to keep in mind it's a slow process."

"Right."

Isaac was nowhere around, but there were signs he'd already eaten: a dish in the sink and a crumpled napkin on the table. Natalie and Jacob stuffed themselves, then were ready to leave.

They ditched their bikes two blocks away from school and circled around to check out the building. One lonely car sat in the parking lot, a navy blue Camry. The school grounds were downright desolate. Since there would be no way to explain wandering around the building on a Saturday night, this was a very good thing, noted Jacob as he unlocked the caretaker's entrance.

"Does your dad know you have that key?" Natalie asked, following him inside.

"Sure. He gave it to me when I was twelve."

"Principal Jefferson hasn't changed the locks in four years?"

Jacob opened his dad's office and rushed down the stairs to the basement, talking quickly over his shoulder, "Why would she? There's hardly any changeover in janitorial staff. The positions are unionized and the same eight guys have worked here the whole time. I think maybe there's one new guy."

She was more than a little surprised to hear that this most basic of security measures hadn't been taken since the string of weird incidents began.

Jacob frantically pulled open drawers in his dad's still-bare desk.

"What are you looking for?" she asked.

"When we entered the school, we triggered the alarm on all the outside doors. I need to disable it before it goes off."

She groaned. "Don't tell me your dad gave you the security password too?"

"Nope." He removed a scrap of paper from a drawer and flashed it in front of her face. "But hacking 101 is anticipating how people *really* use technology."

He made a beeline for a small plastic panel she hadn't noticed next to the cupboard where the intruder had been hiding. He pressed the numbers on the piece of paper and a long beep sounded.

"Phew." He reactivated the alarm and returned the paper to the drawer. "My dad's not supposed to write down the new password every month when they change it. No one is, but I'm willing to bet that Jefferson and the eight janitors who know it have similar papers stashed in completely obvious places. And that includes George Christopheridis, the weekend janitor, who's somewhere in this building—"

"You're one slick bastard," she said, admiringly.

He took a quick bow.

Natalie leaned against the desk and was reminded of something. "Jacob, don't you think it's strange that the only thing the intruder damaged, other than your dad's head, was the computer? I'm just wondering if it could be a clue to what happened." What Natalie didn't say was that she thought Jacob's hacking might be involved.

"Well, I brought the hard drive home to see if I could use it in another box. Maybe I should take a closer look at it first."

"Good idea."

"It only connected to the school network, though. Dad didn't even use it as a personal computer. He's not addicted to the wired universe, like me."

Natalie bit her lip. "What programs could it access over the network?"

Jacob looked away. Natalie wondered for an instant whether his odd expression was guilt. Did he have an idea what the attacker might be after?

"Nothing interesting. The equipment database, the intranet all staff use to stay updated on news..."

"Hmm."

He twisted a knob on the upright cupboard. "Maybe the cached files will tell me something."

"Maybe."

Cutting the conversation short, Jacob pointed at a metal box on the top shelf, above the stacks of paper. "Inside this dinky little safe is a master set of keys that will open every lock in the school."

"All of them?" This was serious business, breaking and entering, but Jacob was fine with "borrowing" his father's keys.

"Yep." He set the box down on his dad's desk, took out his lock-pick set, and went to work.

"How many times have you done this?" she asked, after a few minutes of watching him sweat over the lock.

"Technically? None," he admitted. "I've successfully picked the locks on both my front and back doors. The garage and my dad's car. It takes me awhile. You'll have to be patient, but I'm pretty sure I can open it eventually. It's a three-pin lock. Any ten-year-old could do it."

He acknowledged the absurdity of the school's entire security system being protected by a cheap lockbox with a quick lift of his eyebrows, but didn't take his eyes off his work.

She bent over to watch him work just in time to catch the final twist that released the metal door. He reached in and extracted a honking set of keys the size of his head.

"Sweet," he breathed, making it jangle with a little shake.

"How'll we figure out which one's for Jefferson's office, let alone her filing cabinet?"

"My diligent dad has them all labeled." He indicated tiny little tags affixed to the tops of each key as he flipped through them. They were categorized by color. "Here's the main office doors, including the one to Jefferson's." He unhooked a small ring with about six keys on it. "I'm willing to guess the filing cabinet key's on here too." He put the remaining bulk back into the box, hesitated a second, then shut the door.

"Why'd you do that? You'll just have to pick the lock again when we're done."

"I'd rather not get my dad in trouble, thank you very much," he said, putting the locked box away on the top shelf of the cupboard. "If you're caught poking around in Jefferson's office, and they figure out you got the keys from him, he'd lose his job."

He twisted the box around to make sure it was in exactly the same position he'd found it in, and handed her the keychain. "Well, here you go. Not sure what all the extra keys are for, but the smallish ones look like they might work in filing cabinets or drawers."

She squared her shoulders and took a deep breath, inflating her confidence. Jacob didn't waste any time. He took out the purple toy radios, attached earphones to them, and handed one to her. "Turn it on and keep it in your pocket, out of sight. I'll stay out in the hallway and keep a lookout. We'll use the radio to stay in communication. These babies put me out a whopping $9.99, but they work beautifully." He clipped his to his belt, under his shirt flap. Natalie slipped hers into a pocket and inserted the ear buds.

They left Isaac's office and crept into the school as quietly as possible. It was pitch black. Jacob switched on his flashlight. Natalie cursed the weak light cast by her tiny penlight, which reflected dimly off the lockers on the far wall but barely lit up the floor in front of her.

"We could turn on some lights," said Jacob. "I know where the switches are—but it's better not to risk being seen."

A few steps from the stairs going to the first floor, Jacob put his fingers to his lips. "Shh." He extinguished his light and she did the same. In front of them was an open door with a light on

inside that cut a triangular swath of fluorescence across the hall.

Natalie leaned forward and peered in. A man wearing over-alls was sitting in an office chair, drinking coffee from a ther-mos. His feet were up on a metal desk and a small radio played the golden oldies while he read a tabloid with a cover article about a girl born with three heads. That must be George.

As she crept past the room, Natalie swore George would be able to hear her heart beating. It was so loud it pounded against her ribcage. Somehow, she made it, turned around and watched Jacob's passage. He moved calmly and quickly.

Safely on the other side, he whispered, "George is obvious-ly taking an extended break. Lucky for us. When he goes back to work, he'll most likely clean the second-floor classrooms."

"How do you know?" she whispered.

"I watched him do the whole tour once. My father says I have a brain like a sponge," he said, pushing open the door to the stairwell as slowly as possible, so it wouldn't squeak.

There were low lights on in there and she could see his face clearly for the first time since leaving Isaac's office. He was smirking. "Just admit you couldn't do this without me and all will be well."

"Yes, m'lord."

His smirk turned into a broad grin. "Keep it coming."

A swift elbow to the gut showed him just how likely that was to happen. They took the stairs two at a time, exited into the wide first floor, and plunged back into darkness. The flash-lights snapped back on. As they neared the main office, Jacob took a set of latex gloves out of his pack and gave them to her. "You don't want to leave any fingerprints."

She pulled them on. He momentarily angled his flashlight toward the far side of the hallway, where there was a boys' bathroom. "I'll wait in there with the door open a crack, so I can keep an eye on the hallway."

She nodded and turned to the locked office door. He moved the beam of his light so she could see what she was doing. She inserted the first key on the chain into the lock. They crouched over the doorknob while she fiddled with the lock. Nothing happened.

"Maybe they've changed some of the locks, after all," he said.

She nudged him out of the way.

"Worst comes to worst, I can pick it."

"Hang on a minute. Give me a chance."

"Fine. I just don't want George to decide his break's over while we're standing here."

A soft click sounded. She gave the knob a quick turn. "You were saying?"

He swallowed whatever was on the tip of his tongue and swung his light around to Jefferson's locked office. "One down, two to go."

Wordlessly, she moved forward and inserted the correct key into Jefferson's door. It opened smoothly. She used her tiny penlight to go directly to the cabinet behind the desk. There were eight small keys on the chain and she might have to try them all.

"You can take it from here," said Jacob. "I'm going to the bathroom... err, to keep an eye out for George. Your radio's on, right?"

She paused in the process of examining keys to flick her penlight at the volume on her radio. "Yeah."

"Be careful." He slipped out of the room preceded by a bouncing circle of light, pulling the door closed behind him.

Beads of sweat formed on her forehead. One of the keys finally worked on the cabinet, so she tugged on the drawer. It scraped open noisily.

"What was that?" asked Jacob, over the radio. "I could hear it from here."

"The cabinet needs oil."

"Well, try to keep it down."

"I'm trying."

She sat down cross-legged and thumbed through the folders. There weren't ones for every kid in the school, just those with unusual incidents in their histories. They were filed alphabetically, starting with A, and inside each one, memos, notes and official letters were meticulously entered in chronological order, with the most recent correspondence at the front.

The first interesting file she came across was Sandy Blatchford's. Her two previous reprimands were for showing up at a school function drunk—"student was intoxicated and proceeded to become loud and unruly when teachers requested that she leave"—and for nine straight unexplained absences from history class.

This made Natalie pause to count how many days in a row she'd missed gym, not wanting to bring her spotty attendance record to the attention of Principal Jefferson. Probably not enough to warrant a reprimand.

There was also a note saying that Sandy's legal guardian, her uncle, was none other than Mike Wojcik. Natalie hissed in a breath when she read that. About ten earlier memos dealt with

Sandy's transfer to Western High, three months into grade nine, due to personal problems at home. Prior to being placed in her uncle's custody, she'd temporarily been a ward of the Children's Aid after her mother was arrested for substance abuse.

Feeling a little weird about prying into the personal details of a stranger's life, even if that stranger was responsible for an angry mob of preppy girls chasing her down the street, Natalie clapped the folder shut and put it away. It was strange that someone with a history like that would be so tight with the school's beauty queens. Sandy must be a good enough liar to pretend everything was white picket fences at home.

Her sense of propriety didn't hold her back long, because the next interesting one she grabbed was Eddie Chango's. It was half as thick as Sandy's. In fact, the one and only incident recorded was the expulsion. That was a little odd. Matt had said Eddie was a loose cannon. You'd think at least some of that behavior would have come to the principal's attention.

A four-page typed report by Wojcik had been written the day after he kicked Eddie out of the football game. It detailed Eddie's gradual rage issues during previous practices and the culminating explosion, in the locker room, not on the field, when Eddie swore at the coach and punched him. Wojcik recommended a full expulsion, as opposed to a suspension, in order to avoid future dangerous situations.

The next thing in the file was a short note from Jefferson that suggested lessening Eddie's punishment to a limited expulsion of two months because he'd never been in trouble before. There was a letter recording the date the secretary had submitted the incident report to the school board superintendent. The final memo in the folder was typed by the superintendent's office, and it was his final decision to expel Eddie. Clearly, he'd decided not to be lenient.

Natalie quickly riffled through the other folders, but found nothing on the Hamiltons or Suzy Moon. She did find one with her name on it, though. There was barely anything in it, just a half-page memo detailing Jefferson's conversation with the Brooklyn Heights principal. Yeesh, he'd made it sound like Natalie's parents were fly-by-the-seat-of-their-pants types who didn't have their daughter's academic interests at heart, as opposed to internationally respected journalists. Whatever. Pretty much what she'd expected that dried-up old apple to say.

Jacob had a folder too, with a letter signed by Detective Lewis detailing his arrest, but minimal follow-up on Jefferson's part, since it had happened while he was a student but not on school property. They'd had an informal "discussion" about the sanctity of the school's computer systems. There was nothing in there Natalie didn't already know.

Since she couldn't remember Missy or Lynette's last names, even though Linebacker Lewis had mentioned them during her interrogation, she went back to the beginning of the drawer. As she flipped through the folders, she glanced at the names on them as quickly as possible. She had just found a very thin folder for a Ramiro Lopez that only had one piece of paper in it when the radio crackled in her ear.

"Nat? You there?" said Jacob urgently.

"I'm here," she whispered.

"Hide now," was his muffled response. "Someone's in the hall and it's not George."

Her heart started racing. Did she have time to read the letter in Ramiro's folder?

"He's going toward the office door," hissed Jacob.

She crammed the folder back into the drawer and tried to push it closed. It got stuck, wouldn't shut properly.

"Are you hiding yet? Wait, don't say a word, he's got a key."

Natalie looked around desperately. The only hiding place she could see was underneath Jefferson's big desk.

She scrambled around and pulled her legs up so she was as far back as possible, used her thumb to flick the power switch on her radio so it wouldn't crackle or anything. No sooner had she done that than the office door opened and the lights came on. Heavy footsteps approached and she held her breath.

A pair of men's feet were partially visible under the desk. White lace-up sneakers, but not the same ones the intruder had been wearing. He went to the locked filing cabinet and stooped to tug on the bottom drawer. Assuming it was locked, he yanked so hard the entire cabinet bounced. But it was barely closed, so he flew backward, stumbled and hit the desk. Natalie heard a muffled swear.

She tried to get a better view but couldn't do that without moving and giving herself away. She heard him flipping through the files, and removing one of the folders—it wasn't as thick as Sandy's, could have been Eddie's. Or any number of others.

The man kicked the drawer shut with a bang. Was he trying to alert George? thought Natalie in alarm. He ran across the office and out, slamming the door shut behind him.

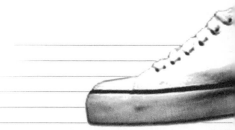

She counted to fifty before turning on her radio. "Is it safe?" she asked.

"There you are!" said Jacob, relief evident in his voice. "Get out now. He went upstairs."

Natalie got to her feet and cautiously inched toward the cabinet.

"Run! I have no idea if he's going to come back."

She wanted to check if the man had taken Eddie's folder, as she suspected, but the drawer was locked again, and she'd have to go through the process of figuring out which key opened it. There was no time. She flicked off the lights and left the office. Jacob immediately materialized in the darkness in front of her and grabbed her hand. They ran down the dark hall together, not daring to turn on their flashlights.

"Did you see his face?" she asked.

"No. He had something over his head."

He tugged her to the right and when they got close to the wall, she saw it was actually a door to the auditorium. She bounded for it, pulled, and it swung open. It seemed even darker in there. She hesitated, but Jacob pulled on her hand and they plunged into the pitch-black room.

"I know my way," he said.

He kept a tight hold on her hand and propelled her forward. She held back, taking more tentative steps, because she didn't like giving up control. This was a new room for her and she had no idea what it looked like with the lights on. When she banged her hip on the back of a row of chairs, she yelped and stopped in her tracks to rub the injury. "Where are you taking me, anyway?"

"There's another staircase."

"Where?"

"Backstage. Let's go."

"I'm in pain here," she said.

Just then, the door they'd come through swung open and light flooded the area nearby. The hall lights were on and a man's shape was framed in the bright doorway. Natalie and Jacob crouched down behind a row of chairs.

"It's George," breathed Jacob next to her ear. "He must have heard you yell when you hurt yourself."

For long moments, George stood there, listening. Finally, he decided there was no one in the auditorium, turned around and left.

Jacob's palm was sweaty when he jerked her up and forward. She moved faster now, as quickly as she could manage. When she stubbed her toe, she didn't even cry out.

"Stairs," warned Jacob, just before the hand that still held hers rose a little. He was already climbing. She cautiously lifted one foot after the other. There were only five steps. They must be onstage. This suspicion was confirmed when they passed through a heavy curtain.

Once they were on the other side, Jacob turned on his flashlight so they could see where they were going. They headed stage left and went down a narrow set of stairs to the basement, passed the empty room where George had been camped out and entered the caretaker's hall.

In his dad's office, Jacob reopened the metal box, hooked the small key chain back onto the set, and did something to the alarm so they would have time to get out of the building

without tripping it. He took her hand again and they ran up the stairs, adrenaline rushing.

They burst outside and the night seemed unbelievably bright in contrast to the thick darkness of the building. To their surprise, Ramiro was in the cranny, alone, drawing in a notebook next to a floodlight with a half-empty bottle of coke next to him. A little boombox was playing Public Enemy's "Fight the Power."

Natalie and Jacob came to a skidding halt. Ramiro looked up and leaned back against one of the mural walls, not at all surprised to see them suddenly appear. His eyes flickered down to their clasped hands and registered curiosity. Jacob suddenly let go, as if she was on fire.

"What are you two lovebirds doing here?" asked Ramiro.

"Not what you think," retorted Natalie. "What are you doing?"

"Needed to get out of the house. My sister moved back in and she's pissing me off. But, hey, I'm not the one who just ran out of a locked building."

Ramiro's story was *way* too convenient. It easily could have been him in the office. Maybe he was stealing his own file or even Eddie's.

Jacob blurted out a version of the truth: "Trying to find out who's behind the attacks on my dad."

"Right... Did you figure it out?"

Natalie cut him off by asking a question. "How well do you know Eddie?"

He put down his notebook. "We're tight. We go way back." His face shut down. "Wait a minute, you think my man's behind this? Where do you get off, Maggie?"

She scowled. "I'm just asking."

He looked away, disgusted.

She pressed forward. "What team's on his MVP watch?"

"Why do you want to know?"

"Humor me."

"Probably the Bears. He has family in Chicago. But how should I know?"

Matt had said he thought it was the Buccaneers, but the Bears' logo was an orange "C." She felt a pang of guilt. It wasn't the right shape or reddish enough to be the attacker's watch. Besides, Eddie had saved her butt last night.

"You really are unbelievable," said Ramiro.

Her anxiety level was still high from the close encounter in Jefferson's office. It didn't take much to lose her patience.

"What's your problem?" she demanded.

"You. You show up at our school and start accusing people of crimes."

"I'm not accusing anyone of anything," she protested, glancing sideways at Jacob, hoping for support. None was forthcoming. "But in the past week, I've stopped a horrible attack, been chased down a deserted street by the Barbie squad, had insults spray-painted on my locker, been fingerprinted by the cops—who, by the way, seem to think I have something to do with a series of crimes that started long before I got to this city—and caught a soccer ball with my face. I just want some answers before I get killed."

Ramiro raised an eyebrow. He still looked pissed. "Well, did you ever stop to think that poking around might destroy a good guy's reputation?"

"Are you talking about yourself or about Eddie? He doesn't have a reputation to destroy. Everyone tells me he's a loose cannon!"

"Who's everyone?" demanded Ramiro.

Natalie wasn't about to point the finger at the Hamiltons. "None of your business."

"Eddie doesn't have many people who'd stick up for him," pitched in Jacob. He looked really uncomfortable. "But then again, neither do I."

"You could also say he's allergic to the authorities," added Ramiro.

"Well, he may have to get over that. From what I can tell, all of Western's problems started around the time Eddie was expelled. Jefferson or Detective Lewis will put two and two together sooner or later."

"Not unless you go opening that big mouth of yours," said Ramiro.

"Jefferson's got her head in the sand anyway," said Jacob.

It annoyed her that Jacob wasn't sticking up for her, so she glared at him, then exhaled slowly and forced herself to calm down. "I'm starting to think Jefferson's less concerned about the incidents that have been happening around here, and more worried about something else."

"No shit, Sherlock," said Jacob.

"Like keeping her precious job!" said Ramiro.

She struggled to keep her temper under control while she figured out what to say. "I'm not sure yet."

"There's no way in hell Eddie'd hurt my dad," piped up Jacob.

"He's solid," agreed Ramiro, holding up his fist for Jacob to punch in solidarity.

She threw her arms in the air. "Fine, I get it. You guys think I'm a jerk for wondering if Eddie's guilty."

"Got a minute for a story, Maggie?" asked Ramiro.

"Sure, I guess," she said.

Ramiro patted the grass. "Have a seat."

chapter ten

 atalie plunked down on the grass and tucked her legs beneath her. Beside her, Jacob slid his pack of equipment off his shoulder and sank to his knees.

"It's about Eddie," Ramiro said, licking his lips as if he had to gear himself up for the long tale. "It's really his story to tell, but I figure that since you're, like, some kind of girl detective and you're poking around in his business, he's safer if you find out his dirty secrets from me than from a teacher or some cop."

"Let's hear it," she said, waving a hand impatiently.

"My man Eddie has had a hard life—hey, look around, so have all of us—but he's had it even worse. His parents moved here from Cuba when he was three. Now he lives with his kid brother Nelson in a basement apartment five blocks from here. Nelson's fourteen. They had an older sister too. Her name was Jenny. Four years ago, Jenny disappeared. She was in a bad headspace, turning tricks down on Queen Street for cash. One night some guy picked her up, took her out to the Scarborough Bluffs and killed her."

Natalie regretted being snappy earlier.

"As you would expect, after that, Eddie's family fell apart. His mom found religion in a serious way. His dad started

drinking worse and worse. One day he left for work and never came home. It tore his mother away from reality. She started to forget things, like who her sons were and why she should get out of bed in the morning. It was spooky."

Natalie shuddered, thinking about the shouting matches her parents had had for a few months before the separation. There hadn't been any physical violence, but there was always the threat that someone might go too far, the terrifying possibility that things could spin out of control. Maybe all long-term relationships eventually drowned in painful memories.

"Eddie's mom brought home a new guy, who started knocking her around. Eddie kept getting in the middle of it, trying to protect his mom. Told people the bruises were from football practice. One day when the old man went after Nelson with a broomstick, Eddie grabbed his brother and ran. They only had the clothes on their backs. Stayed at my folks' place for a couple days, then found a room in some boarding house downtown and went on welfare to pay the rent. What with taking care of his brother and doing homework, it became really hard for Eddie to make football practice. He was stretched thin."

"Wow, all this happened last year?" asked Natalie.

"Yep. Mr. Marsden, the old coach, had a soft spot for my man. Felt for him. Marsden was like that. Knew what was going on at home and that Eddie was letting out steam on the field. Didn't hurt that Eddie could do no wrong. He was like a man possessed, ya know?"

Natalie nodded. She could wrap her brain around the game when she thought of it like that.

"But then Marsden retired at the end of last season and

Wojcik stepped up as coach. Suddenly, Eddie went from junior MVP to favorite whipping boy. Literally. Nobody could figure it out. Wojcik would scream at him in front of everyone, face red, crazy spit flying out of the sides of his mouth. One day, in the locker room, he reached over and grabbed Eddie by the shoulder to turn him around and make him listen. It brought back too many memories for Eddie. He pushed the coach's arm away a little harder than he'd meant to, and Wojcik fell over. A couple guys were there. They *saw* Eddie had a sweater in one hand and some Gatorade in the other—he wasn't picking a fight. But Wojcik stood up, told them to go home for the day, and marched right into Jefferson's office. Just like that, Eddie was expelled."

It took a moment for Natalie to realize he'd finished his story. She'd been so still while she listened that it was like the air was sucked right out of her. Ramiro's account of what happened was so different from Wojcik's official report. And if a couple other guys saw what happened, why didn't they...

Suddenly a car squealed out of the staff parking lot, breaking the spell. All three of them turned to watch the navy blue sedan Natalie had assumed was George's whip down the street, burning rubber. It slowed down momentarily as it passed the bike area, then picked up speed. Natalie squinted to see the driver but the car was moving too fast.

"I need Eddie's number," she said to Ramiro.

"What for?" he asked suspiciously. The walls were back up.

"I want to ask him some stuff."

"How about I give you his email?" Without waiting for her consent, he picked up his artist's notebook and took a black

Sharpie out of his pocket. Ramiro had pasted a painting by Keith Haring onto the book's cover. Natalie had seen a big Haring show in New York a few years back. He was one of the first graffiti artists to make it big and used his simplistic, cartoony style to comment on political issues. Not a bad role model for a muralist. Ramiro flipped past pages of drawings to find an empty sheet, jotted down the email address in his jagged stylized script and handed it to her.

"I've got to head," said Ramiro, standing up. He started to walk away, then turned back to Natalie. "Better yet, you lovebirds should come downtown tomorrow, to this huge graffiti expo that's happening. I'll be throwing up a mural and Eddie's gonna be there."

"Gracias, Che," she said, following the Argentine custom of calling everyone "guy."

To her astonishment, he actually laughed. "Maggie, how'd you guess my middle name?"

"What, you mean Loser?" she teased. There was no anger behind her words; she was trying to lighten up the mood.

He raised one eyebrow.

"Seriously," she said. "I have no idea what you're talking about."

"It's Ernesto. After Ernesto 'Che' Guevara. He's my old man's idol."

"My dad's too," said Natalie.

Ramiro leaned forward and lifted a fist. Natalie realized he was waiting for her to punch it back and she was absurdly touched by this sign he'd welcomed her into his group of friends.

They split up. Natalie walked with Jacob back to their bikes and while they rode to her place, she told him everything she'd discovered in Jefferson's locked filing cabinet. She started up her driveway, still gabbing, then realized he'd stopped back at the curb, resting on one foot. She wanted to invite him in, but her father would ask too many questions.

"Thanks for everything, Jacob. We make a good team."

"No probs."

"I guess I'll see you later."

"Later," he said, miles away. He pushed off the curb and pedaled away, wiry frame winding from side to side. She watched him for a few seconds, wondering what was on his mind, before carrying her bike onto the porch and heading inside.

Opening the door to the basement stairs, she yelled down: "Dad, you still alive down there?"

"*Si, Nati,*" was the muffled reply.

"Ever coming out?"

"Soon."

She poured herself a glass of fizzy water and sat down at the counter to wait. Her father eventually climbed the stairs, wiping his hands on a soft cloth.

"I lost track of time," he said, as if she didn't already know that.

Her father could play in his darkroom for days on end. If nobody interrupted him, he'd only surface to make a sandwich or a cup of coffee. It was one of the sore points between him and Brenda. When things were good, she'd called him focused and driven. When they got bad, she said he was on some other planet.

Jorge squinted at the clock on the stove and realized it was close to ten. "Have you been out all this time?"

"Got back a little while ago," she said, vaguely.

"Ahh. So what did you do all night?" he asked.

"Hung out with Jacob."

"Tell me about this boy."

"Dad!" she protested.

"What?" He was all innocence as he poured himself some water from the bottle Natalie'd taken from the fridge. "If he's going to be spending that much time with my daughter, I should know more about him."

"He's a total computer geek."

Her dad looked amused. "That's the most fascinating thing you can think to tell me about a boy you just spent the entire evening with? He has great prowess with machines?"

"He's in my geography class," she added lamely, casting around for a way to change the topic of conversation. "So, can you send Mom's present for me?"

Her father nodded. He was smart enough to figure out exactly what she was doing, but kind enough to let her get away with it. "And you'll call her, right?"

"Sure," she said, draining her glass of water. "I'm going to bed. Don't stay up too late. It can't be good for you to be inhaling all those chemicals for so long."

He chuckled. "Haven't killed me yet."

Groaning, she tried to imagine what it would be like to live with her mother. She'd probably spend a lot of time alone in hotels around the world, playing computer solitaire. At least her dad surfaced from his darkroom sometimes. She pushed

the thought from her mind and trekked upstairs to her room.

Sunday morning, she made a big show of doing homework and helping out around the house, so her father wouldn't try to stop her from going to Ramiro's graffiti show in the afternoon. Jorge made her promise to be home for dinner—he was ordering Chinese—but otherwise didn't complain. It helped that he was back in the basement.

She changed into jeans and a dark green top with a wide neckline that hung down off one shoulder, swiped on some lip gloss and left the house. As she walked down the front path, she heard whistling from one of the Hamiltons' second-floor windows. Ruth and Suzy called out that they were coming down.

"We're studying for a history quiz," said Ruth as they burst out of the door.

Suzy winked exaggeratedly. "Studying really hard."

Natalie grinned. "You are such keeners."

"That's what my parents said this morning, when I told them how I'd be spending the afternoon."

"Where you going?" asked Ruth.

"To check out a mural Ramiro's painting at some graffiti expo downtown."

"You're friends with that guy now?" asked Ruth. "I hear he's already been arrested twice for tagging."

"Hate to tell you this, but he's best buds with your lover boy," said Suzy.

"That's how I met him," confirmed Natalie.

"Jacob's not my lover boy," growled Ruth. "But he does have odd taste in friends."

"And girls," joked Suzy.

"Shut up," said Ruth. "You don't know what you're talking about."

"Bye. Have fun," said Natalie, feeling conflicted about that hand-holding moment with Jacob as she crossed the grass. What would Ruth do if she found out? Would she be devastated? A streetcar came and Natalie hopped on it.

The expo consisted of maybe a hundred people milling around twenty or so partially painted murals in a big parking lot. Big signs proclaimed that the expo was sponsored by a spray paint company and the advertising firm that created giant murals on buildings around town. The organizers had erected blank plywood surfaces and several local businesses along the alley behind the lot had offered up their walls.

As she entered the fray, someone stuffed a pamphlet with a map into her hand. Ram666's mural had been given a prominent location, visible from the sidewalk on the far side of the lot. Local artists were working on the plywood and big-name out-of-towners created works on the walls that wouldn't disappear as soon as the event was over. She slowly wound her way there, stopping to watch the artists apply one color layer at a time, in broad strokes that were only discernible as shapes when she stood back a ways.

One of them showed a dance club in a detailed panorama complete with a frenetic crowd, a DJ spinning records, go-go dancers, bartenders showing off for tips, and a line-up for the bathroom. The people—fat, skinny, short, tall, white, black, male, female—were each blissed out in their own little world. Another mural was a cityscape, which transformed the buildings into monsterlike creatures that looked like they might

swallow the people and cars in their shadows. Behind them, the sky was an unnatural rainbow of colors, and at their feet, weeds sprouted bravely through cracks in the cement.

She eventually found Ramiro's mural. The little pamphlet said it honored the Day of the Dead, a traditional Mexican holiday. The white outlines of mischievous *calaveras*—skeletons—leered and danced merrily around the edges. But Ramiro had subverted it and turned it into a shrine to his Chilean ancestors on both sides of the family—clusters of Spanish and indigenous faces.

At first, he didn't notice her standing there because he was absorbed in his work and wearing an enormous gas mask to protect himself from the fumes. It looked as if he was re-creating a small-scale drawing done in his notepad on the enormous canvas.

When a guy wearing a volunteer badge stopped by to offer him a sports drink, Ramiro put down his aerosol can, removed his face mask for a breather, wiped his brightly painted hands on a rag, and accepted the drink with a nod. As soon as the volunteer walked away, Ramiro scanned the crowd.

When he noticed Natalie standing there, his face brightened and he indicated for her to come hang out with him. "Hey, Maggie. You're looking hot today. What's the occasion?"

"No occasion," she said, accepting the dubious compliment for what it was.

He bounced anxiously and took a gulp from the bottle in his hand. "I always get nervous when I'm in front of a crowd. I'm used to working alone."

"Your mural's incredible."

Ramiro pinched her cheek. "Thanks, Maggie."

"You're lucky it's so amazing, or I would have to kill you for that."

He pretended to be scared.

"So, where are your friends? I thought they'd be here, cheering you on."

He scowled. "Those guys took off for a bite an hour and a half ago. Haven't seen them since. They're supposed to have my back. Riiight."

He pulled his gas mask back on, picked up a can of green spray paint, and started to fill in some grass with short, repetitive strokes. Since the stool wasn't occupied, she claimed it. Perched on top, she pulled out her notebook and made a list of all the unexplained events that were jumbled in her head. When she next raised her head, the parking lot had filled up as shoppers stopped to find out what was going on.

Her pamphlet had little paragraphs about the artists on the back. She discovered Ramiro was one of the founding members of the Graffiti Transformation Project, which painted community murals on schools and community centers that commissioned them. Some of the other artists looked interesting too. She was considering wandering around to check out the work she hadn't seen yet when Ramiro pulled off his mask again and said, "Screw you guys."

For once, he wasn't annoyed with her. Eddie and three other guys, including Jacob, had just walked up. Jacob smiled at Natalie, but when he looked away his mouth drooped back into a frown. Something was on his mind, but she decided not to worry about it.

Eddie jostled Ramiro with a broad shoulder, his exuber-

ance at odds with his tough-guy exterior. He wore a white shirt with cut-off sleeves that showed his tattoo and baggy jeans held up by a wide leather belt. His face shone, showing how chuffed he was at the attention Ramiro was getting.

"So, man, how does it feel to be famous?" Eddie winked while he spoke.

"Wouldn't know," retorted Ramiro, sourly.

"Soon they'll be throwing money at ya," said Eddie.

It was impossible to stay annoyed with that. Ramiro cracked, grinning despite his irritation.

"Don't worry, we all know you're a sell-out," said Eddie.

"Shut up," said Ramiro, pretending to spray-paint Eddie's face.

Natalie decided Ramiro was eighteen going on eight. And she noticed that Jacob was still studiously avoiding her eyes. Maybe all boys were.

Ramiro went back to work and the two friends Natalie didn't know took off to see how the other murals had progressed while they were eating.

"Any chance I can talk to you, Eddie?" asked Natalie.

"I'm here."

She made a face. "I mean alone. Let's go for a walk."

Eddie mugged a lecherous face for his friends' benefit, but followed her through the parking lot and across the street. He sat down on a waist-high slab of cement facing the crowd but far enough away to speak confidentially.

"Eddie, I know this is probably the last thing you want to talk about, but can you tell me what happened between you and Wojcik?"

Eddie kicked a rock on the sidewalk. "I'm trying to forget about that guy."

"I'm so sorry for bringing it up. It's just that... I think there should have been an investigation into the complaint he made about you."

"How do you know about that?"

"I have my ways," she said evasively.

His eyes narrowed. "Damn straight there should have been some kind of investigation." He crossed his arms and hunched over to stare at his feet. The bicep closest to her was bulging, which made his tattoo stand out. It was a football.

"Why wasn't there one?"

"Because I'm a poor black kid and he's a white teacher." Air hissed out between his teeth as he struggled to keep his voice under control. "The system's corrupt. Teachers are like cops, man, their word is the law."

"Did you ask Principal Jefferson to look into the incident?"

"Sure. The letter they sent me said to stay five hundred metres away from school property, so all I could do was call and leave messages. She wouldn't even talk to me. Her secretary told me to save my breath for the superintendent. He was supposed to call and get my side of the story."

"But he never did."

Eddie bent his head, struggling with emotion. "Well, he called. Asked about five questions and barely listened to my answers. I could tell he'd already made up his mind. And I missed a job interview to sit around waiting for that call too. What a scam. I wanted him to know the truth, that Wojcik had

it in for me from the moment he started coaching, but that guy didn't hear a word I said."

"That sucks."

"Jefferson's the one I'm really pissed at. I mean, she's known me for years and I'd never done anything like this before. But she wouldn't even take ten minutes to deal with my situation. I used to think she was a fair principal, you know?"

"She should have looked into it. Talked to the guys who witnessed the incident."

"Damn right. I left her a bunch of messages. All I know's football was my whole life and I was doing fine in school. Now I have nothing."

"Do you think Jefferson might have had some reason for avoiding the situation? Something that fits into the bigger picture?"

Eddie stood up angrily and spat on the ground. "What bigger picture? My life has been ruined. What's bigger than that?"

He stalked off. Instead of going back to the mural, Natalie walked the short distance to the streetcar stop. To her surprise, Jacob came running up while she was waiting.

"Hey," he said, almost shyly. "What did Eddie say?"

"Apparently, he asked Jefferson to take a closer look at Wojcik's report, but she never got back to him."

"Figures. She probably just wanted to brush it under the rug."

"I guess."

A streetcar pulled up to the stop. Jacob pressed something into her palm.

She looked down and discovered it was a cell phone.

Plugged into it was a small little device that looked like a metal barrette. "Thanks, but I already have a cell."

"This one's special. It's Bluetooth technology. That little clip's a microphone you can attach to your shirt or the strap of your bag. Just hit redial and the phone will automatically connect to my computer, which is set up to record. Think of it as leaving me a really long voice mail."

"Why are you giving me this?"

"It will pick up conversations, even if you're just talking normally."

She still didn't really understand. "Why would I need it?"

"I'm worried that your poking around could... That you might be in serious danger."

"Um... Okay. Thanks. Hey, is anything else wrong?"

He looked away. "What do you mean?"

"You're acting all distant."

"It's just a little much for me... all of this. I don't trust people easily."

"Neither do I."

The streetcar lurched to a halt in front of them and the doors banged open. She paid and turned to wave through a window, but Jacob was already shuffling off into the crowd.

chapter eleven

 atalie rode to school with the Hamiltons bright and early on Monday, feeling the effects of a guilty conscience and expecting someone to have figured out that she and Jacob broke into Jefferson's office. It would serve her right to get caught. Not that she was going to turn herself in or anything.

As they were locking up, a group of blonde girls came around the side of the school and Natalie flashed back to the mob on Friday night—tight clothing, makeup, blonde hair and mean grins. Missy and Lynette were among this group, but not Sandy.

Following the rules of high school social interaction, the Golden Girls shouldn't be treating Natalie this way anymore. She was friends with their leader's boyfriend. Unless, of course, the bullying was personal, not just a rite of passage for the new girl. Had she stepped on their pedicured toes again in some way?

She'd been so busy watching the blondes and tuning out Ruth and Matt, who'd been bickering ever since they left the house, that she almost didn't hear a familiar voice call out, "Hey, Maggie! My man Eddie needs to talk to you."

She turned to see Ramiro climb out of Eddie's car, which

was parked halfway up on the sidewalk. She walked over and bent down to peer at Eddie through the open car window. "You're not supposed to be here."

Eddie leaned into the passenger seat and winked. "I'm not on school grounds. This sidewalk is public property. I'm a tax-paying citizen. Technically, I own it."

She rolled her eyes. "You're not five hundred metres away, though."

Eddie let out a hiss of air between his teeth. "Pfft. I'll respect their rules the day they actually listen to my side of the story. Anyway, I just stopped by to give you this." He passed her Wojcik's report—he had no idea she'd already read it in his confidential student file. "I made you a copy. Read it for yourself. You'll see how messed up the situation is."

"Thanks, I will."

She straightened up and discovered that Ramiro was staring down Missy and crew, who were now over with Matt and Ruth. Natalie wouldn't want to be on the receiving end of that look.

"Chill," she said.

"Those girls aren't still out for blood?" he asked.

"Not at the moment. But they might start up again if you don't stop staring like that. Sandy's not even over there. I wish I could figure out what her problem is."

"You'll find out, sooner or later."

"Great."

"You'd just better hope I'm around when you do."

Eddie called out from inside the car: "For now, why don't you just go to class? At least *you're* allowed into the school."

"Already gone," said Natalie, slipping the report into her

bag and walking up toward the school with Ramiro. When they passed the Hamiltons, he gave a curt nod in their direction.

Just then, Sandy jogged by and entered the school alone without even glancing at her friends. Missy looked confused, as if she didn't know why Sandy was giving her the cold shoulder. Natalie muttered a quick goodbye to Ramiro and jogged to the door. She slipped through just in time to see Sandy turn left down the main hallway. There were tons of students around, because it was just before nine. Natalie surreptitiously took out the phone Jacob had given her, clipped on the mic, and hit autodial to start recording.

"Hey, Sandy," she yelled, picking up speed.

Sandy's blonde hair whipped around. She groaned when she saw who it was.

Natalie forced her fake smile a little wider when she caught up to the girl.

"Perfect. The little Spic who's ruining my life."

"What did you just call me?"

"A Spic," spat Sandy.

A girl running in the opposite direction gasped at Sandy's name-calling, but didn't slow down. She slipped into a classroom with an apologetic glance in Natalie's direction.

"I see," said Natalie, refusing to lose her temper because Sandy was lashing out like a cornered animal. Come to think of it, maybe Missy and Lynette didn't have a hate on for her. Maybe the problem was always just Sandy. "How exactly am I ruining your life?"

"Just stay the hell away from me," snarled Sandy.

"You were working alone, weren't you? I mean, the soccer

ball in gym class was sort of a group effort, but it was your idea. You spray-painted my locker without Missy and Lynette's help. They have no idea. And I bet you didn't mention that your band of cronies tried to jump me on Friday night, either."

"You're just lucky your pet thugs showed up," said Sandy, darting to one side.

Natalie neatly blocked her path. "My 'pet thugs' really have it in for you."

Some nearby students looked over and tittered. Natalie was causing a scene. She didn't care.

Sandy stopped trying to get past when she realized her only option was to physically move Natalie out of the way. One on one, she was the weaker. "I just wanted to make sure you got the message."

"What message?"

Sandy's face was pale with rage. "Leave Western alone. Stop poking around. Go away! What happens here is none of your business!"

"As if. I'm stuck with this city and a school where people hate me before they give me a chance. What did I ever do to you?"

"You don't understand."

"Then explain it. I'm not stupid."

Any remaining color in Sandy's face drained away. When she spoke again, her voice was significantly subdued. "You're getting involved in a dangerous... Just leave me alone."

"Why should I?" demanded Natalie.

Suddenly, Sandy went limp. Her shoulders sagged and her lip quavered. Tears welled up in her eyes, she covered her face with her hand and shook with a wracking sob. Natalie took a surprised step backward. Either the girl was a really good actor or she was on the verge of a breakdown.

"Talk to me," said Natalie.

"I'm s-so sorry," blubbered Sandy. She spun around and ran out of the school.

Natalie stood there for a few seconds, bewildered. Turning off her phone, she wondered whether Jacob would have any idea what Sandy was talking about when he listened to the recording. What was Sandy involved in that she had to protect so fiercely? Rather than making Natalie want to back off, all the warnings just made her feel encouraged that she was getting close to figuring this out.

Natalie's brain finally kicked in and she headed to gym. Soccer turned out to be a remarkably pleasant experience without Sandy there. Missy and Lynette were, but with the exception of a less than thrilled head nod while they took defensive positions on the opposing team, they ignored her.

Natalie was on offence this time. She drilled a couple of balls into their poorly defended net, earning the oblivious defenders some dirty looks from their teammates and a reprimand from Ms. Marshall: "Missy, Lynette. Look alive!"

After class, Natalie walked toward the change room, mopping her forehead with the bottom of her T-shirt, when Ms. Marshall called her over. The teacher was dragging one of the goals into a storeroom. "Ms. Fuentes, I see you decided to join us today."

Natalie looked at the teacher, unsure what to say.

Ms. Marshall waved a hand at the opposite end to indicate

that Natalie should help her out. Natalie lifted her side and they carried it off the floor.

"Cat got your tongue? I thought maybe you'd dropped the class."

The gym teacher seemed like the type of person who played it straight. "Look, Ms. Marshall, I'm sorry. It's not like me to skip classes, I swear. I just had to... make sure it was safe for me to return."

"Safe," Ms. Marshall's expression indicated she knew exactly what Natalie meant, but was making up her own mind whether Natalie's attendance might turn out to be an ongoing problem. "I couldn't help noticing that the day you show up, Sandy Blatchford is absent."

"With all due respect, that's my business," said Natalie.

Ms. Marshall's lips tightened into a hard line. Oops. That was the wrong thing to say.

"When your business is affecting your ability to show up at my class, it becomes mine too. You get marked on participation, Natalie. Not to mention the fact that I'm obligated to raise such issues with Principal Jefferson."

"I'd appreciate it if you didn't do that," said Natalie, biting her lip. "From now on, I'll be here every day. In fact, I'll be early and stay to help out at the end."

Ms. Marshall held up a warning finger. "One more chance, Natalie. That's it. If you miss a single class for the rest of the semester, I'll report all your absences to the principal."

"I won't let you down," said Natalie, hoping it was true.

The teacher nodded curtly, and carried the bundled-up net into her office.

Natalie heaved a sigh of relief and went into the change room to throw on her clothes. She ran to geography class, feeling slightly giddy she'd managed to weasel out of another crisis. One of her favorite indie cartoonists drew a strip about Crisis Girl, a superhero who used crisis energy to solve dilemmas, and sold screen-printed T-shirts at zine fairs. Next time she saw him, she'd buy one.

She slid into the classroom two minutes late. Thirty sets of eyes watched her slink to the back of the room. Jacob was already there, but when she looked at him, he gave a distant half-smile and turned to face the teacher again. At the end of class, he rushed out the door before she could say a word.

Wishing she could have talked to him about Sandy, she gathered her books and went out to the courtyard to find Ruth and Suzy, taking a route past Jefferson's office. She'd seen an episode of *CSI* once where the detectives said that arsonists often return to the scene of the crime to see the results of their work. That's how she felt, peering into the office as she passed.

The principal was actually standing outside it, chatting with a small group of official-looking men. One of them caught Natalie's eye. He was dressed expensively, in a suit tailored to fit his tall frame. He didn't look much over fifty, but was well on his way to bald, just a few hardy gray hairs combed over his crown.

To say he was furious wouldn't be a stretch, Natalie decided after she caught a few words that came out of his mouth. She paused at a water fountain to eavesdrop.

"This is highly irresponsible, June," he said, voice vibrating with emotion. "You know better. You're the principal of this school—in charge of over two thousand kids and a staff of eighty. Crack down and let them know who's boss!"

"I hear you. But I've almost resolved the situation..."

"Almost doesn't cut it, June," he barked.

Jefferson winced. "Things aren't as bad they seem. I mean..."

"If anything else goes missing, I'll be forced to take matters into my own hands. Your students don't respect you, or they wouldn't be stealing things from right under your nose."

"I'm not certain that the equipment *has* been stolen," Jefferson squeezed out. Her fists were balls of tension at her sides. "Last time, some of it reappeared a few days after it went missing."

"What, you're telling me someone's just borrowing it?"

"Well, without permission."

"Are you seriously suggesting someone would go through all the trouble to sneak into the school at night in order to borrow some sweaty uniforms? And I suppose a little gremlin broke into your filing cabinets?"

A muscle twitched in the principal's cheek. "My filing cabinet's another matter."

Natalie straightened with a jerk, causing Jefferson to notice her for the first time. The principal's eyes narrowed. Yikes! Natalie dried her mouth with the back of her hand and hurried off before she could draw any more attention to herself.

Out in the courtyard, Suzy had her nose in a Catwoman comic. Ruth lay on her back on a bench nearby.

"You guys will never believe what I just saw," said Natalie, as she approached.

Suzy tilted her head to one side inquiringly.

"Jefferson was getting bawled out by some suit in front of everybody."

"Who was he?" asked Ruth.

"Don't know. A bald guy."

"I bet it was her boss," said Suzy, clucking her tongue. "None other than school board superintendent Samuel T. Winthrop. I saw him and his cronies pull up in a BMW while I was in science class this morning."

"He said that if she didn't take care of the situation here, he'd have to handle it himself. It was like he enjoyed humiliating her. You should have heard him yelling."

"Doesn't surprise me," said Suzy. "I've heard about that guy. He's pretty conservative and a bit of an old boy."

Ruth added, "He probably isn't too happy that the largest school in his district is run by a woman."

Ruth and Suzy pulled out their bagged lunches. Natalie'd forgotten their Monday routine. She wished she'd brought her own. "I need to eat something. All I had for breakfast was a granola bar."

"Let's go to the caf," said Suzy.

"Cheap and dirty," said Ruth.

Even a cardboard sandwich would have sounded tempting. Natalie was that starving.

Just as they entered the cafeteria, Ruth barreled into Jacob, who was leaving with a slice of pizza. The slice slipped off the paper plate he was carrying. He dived and caught it by the crust in his other hand. A little cheese and tomato sauce oozed off the bottom. He caught that with the paper plate.

"Smooth moves," said Suzy, admiringly.

"Th-thanks."

"I'm so sorry," gushed Ruth, blushing.

"Don't worry about it."

The three girls had unintentionally surrounded him. He glanced from one to the other, then at the door behind them. He stepped back and hit the wall. He had nowhere to run.

"Why don't you come sit with us?" asked Ruth, taking a step forward.

His eyes flickered to Natalie, who schooled her face to show no emotion. She didn't care whether or not he joined them. At least, she didn't want him to know she did.

"All right," he said.

They went into the cafeteria. Natalie lined up for food while the others went to find seats. When she rejoined them, Jacob had finished his slice. Natalie put down her hot dog, fries and a slice of blueberry pie with whipped topping.

Ruth grabbed a fry before Natalie could even sit. "We told him what you saw outside the office."

"Well, it's not my only news," said Natalie, telling them about her earlier conversation with Sandy.

"She's psycho," said Ruth, eyes wide.

"She admitted she's behind everything?" asked Jacob.

"Kind of. It was weird. We didn't get into specifics, but yeah, I can pretty much chalk up my past week's torture to her."

"She's probably the one who's stealing stuff too," said Suzy.

"It's not just thefts," said Jacob. "There were other things, like a couple broken windows, and these stickers that make fun

of Jefferson and some of the teachers. I only know about it all because my dad's in charge of cleaning up. The stickers were the worst. He had to go around scraping at them for hours."

Natalie stuffed the last bite of hot dog into her mouth, pulled over the pie and dug in. "I don't think she's responsible for that. But I'm starting to have a theory."

"Spill!" said Suzy.

"Not until I'm sure. I don't want to get anyone in trouble," said Natalie, grabbing a napkin. Next to her, Jacob was staring at her—whether because of her ability to demolish such a huge quantity of food in less than five minutes or her pronounce-ment, she was unsure.

"I want to be sure before I accuse anyone," she said.

Jacob nodded in agreement, probably thinking about how angry Ramiro got when she suggested Eddie might be respon-sible for the crimes.

"Well, then, what's your next move?" asked Suzy. "Or is that top secret too?"

"Nah. I need to talk to the superintendent. I'm going to surprise him at his office after school."

"Alone?" asked Ruth, fretting. "I have dance class."

"I can come," said Suzy, frowning. "But my mother needs me to work at the store at five. We're getting a huge shipment of envelopes. Wa-hoo."

"I'll come too," said Jacob. "And don't forget to use the cell phone."

Natalie patted her ever present canvas bag. "I already did that once today, when I was talking to Sandy."

Jacob explained to the other girls that Natalie could record conversations using the phone. "The batteries might be a little low, since I forgot to give you the recharger. I'll take it into my dad's office and plug it in. I can grab it at the end of the day."

Natalie handed it over. "Thanks."

Jacob balled up the paper plate that had held his slice. "Let's meet near the bikes after last period."

"Fine," she said, shrugging.

He put on his headphones and tossed his garbage in a bin near the door on his way out.

"Someone's worried about Natalie's safety," said Suzy, wiggling her eyebrows.

"Does he like you?" asked Ruth, a little more soberly.

She didn't look too upset, but Natalie wasn't comfortable with the direction this conversation was headed. Ruining her brand-new friendship was the last thing she wanted. Still, truth was the best policy.

"I don't know," she said, shaking her head. She pictured them holding hands and running through the halls in the dark, and sighed. "One minute he's my new best friend, the next he seems to hate me."

"He doesn't hate you," said Ruth.

Jacob didn't like her—that way—did he? "Who knows?"

"It's pretty obvious."

"I guess. Anyway, I can't be late for math class. Let's get out of here." They headed out of the cafeteria. "I'll see you later, Suzy."

Natalie split from her friends, got her math and English books from her locker and arrived in class a few minutes before anyone else. She was reviewing the homework when Mr. Wojcik entered the room.

He closed the door behind himself and it clicked shut. They were completely alone.

He threw the stack of papers in his arms onto his desk, side-stepped student desks as he wound over to where she was sitting, and rested one hand on the pages of her open book. "What did you say to my niece this morning?"

Natalie glanced at the door, hoping someone would come in. "Sandy? Um, nothing."

"You better watch out. You're new here," he said.

She pushed her chair backward. "I... I don't understand."

"I'm your teacher. I deserve a little respect. I know your type, with your dyed hair and tough-girl earrings. You've been nothing but trouble since you showed up."

Natalie opened her mouth to protest. Just then, there was a tap at the door and a student's head peered through the window. One of the jocks. Wojcik must have locked it when he came in. He leaned right over her desk and hissed, "Get out of my classroom."

"Sorry?"

"Get the hell out, now! Move it. I don't want to see your face."

She practically leaped out of her chair. Wojcik went over, unlocked the door and yanked it open. Students poured in, looking perturbed. Natalie collected her stuff as quickly as possible. She shook as she bolted out of the room, and through the halls to her locker. Sliding down to the ground, she tried to breathe calmly.

Why would Wojcik be so furious with her? They'd barely had any contact with each other. Maybe there was a bigger

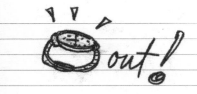

issue here. Something that connected his lies in his report about Eddie to his niece's behavior. Now, more than ever, she knew she was close to resolving the mystery. Wojcik was intimidating, but not enough to make her back off.

chapter twelve

fter twenty minutes, Natalie dragged her sorry butt off the floor and started pacing through the halls, which were empty because everyone was supposed to be in class. She wandered out to the bike nook, but no one was around. The day was windy and overcast, and the fresh air felt cleansing. Her mood started to pick up.

It would be much easier to catch the school superintendent here than to try to get into his office for a meeting, she realized, wondering whether he was still around. Since she had nothing better to do, she made her way around the building's perimeter toward the parking lot. The shiny BMW Suzy had seen in the morning stuck out like a sore thumb amidst the teachers' more humble SUVs and hatchbacks.

She decided to camp out on the slope heading down to the lot and hope he would retrieve his car before it was time for her English class.

Sure enough, fifteen minutes later, the school doors opened and the three men who were talking to Jefferson that morning came out. She leaped up and ran over.

"Mr. Winthrop?" she asked breathlessly, cursing the fact that she'd given Jacob the cell.

"And you are..?" interjected a man with spectacles who hovered next to Winthrop.

"Natalie Fuentes. I need to speak with you for a moment."

"Regarding...?" said the man.

"The outstanding incident that occurred here last spring."

"And that incident would be...?"

Natalie looked away, belatedly realizing that Winthrop had probably been informed of several incidents at the school. "The expulsion of a student named Eddie Chango. Eddie filed a complaint about the process, but that doesn't seem to have been followed up."

"I remember the incident, young lady," boomed Winthrop, speaking for the first time. "The boy who attacked his football coach."

For visual effect, Natalie took Eddie's report from her bag and waved it in his face. She had to reach up—he was quite a bit taller than her. Tall enough to be the attacker? Yeesh, now she was suspecting every man who came near her: Ramiro, Eddie, Jacob, Wojcik, Winthrop... "I have it on good authority that two eye witnesses are willing to testify something completely different than the event Mr. Wojcik reported."

Winthrop's eyes narrowed suspiciously. "How'd you get that report?"

Natalie stifled a highly inappropriate nervous urge to giggle. She confessed: "I'm a friend of Eddie's. But that doesn't change the fact that there are two very different versions of the event floating around."

"You're trying to tell me you think Mike Wojcik falsified his report? Why on earth would he do that?"

"Maybe to get Eddie thrown out of school?"

"Wasn't he the best player on the football team? That doesn't make any sense."

"Mr. Winthrop, I don't know *why* he did it. I just want you to reopen Eddie's case and ask the two guys who were there what they saw."

"I'm sorry, but I can't afford to question every decision I make. And there's altogether too much violence in our schools. I'm sure you agree with me. I simply cannot be lenient about this kind of aggressive behavior." Winthrop took three long strides toward his vehicle, then paused to throw over his shoulder: "I suggest you go back inside and focus on your own studies!"

His underlings rushed to catch up.

"Mr. Wojcik just threw me out of class for no reason," yelled Natalie, kicking herself as soon as the words were out of her mouth for the lame retort. "I'm getting close to the truth and when I do, I'm going to blow this wide open. If Eddie's expulsion wasn't handled appropriately, he deserves another chance."

That stopped Winthrop—and his aides. They turned back to her. Winthrop's look indicated she was giving him a serious headache. He reached for the report.

"Fine. I'll look into it," he said.

"Is that a promise?"

He frowned but nodded slightly. "Now, if you'll excuse me, I have work waiting."

Natalie headed back into the school, a little early for English, but satisfied with herself. She had to work hard to pay attention to the class. When the final bell rang, she ran out to find Suzy and Jacob, and give them the update.

"Guess we don't have to sneak into his office," said Suzy.

"He actually agreed to take another look at Eddie's case?" asked Jacob, dubiously.

Natalie nodded. "That's right. And I'm going to make sure he doesn't forget."

"The thorn in his side," teased Suzy.

"You're amazing," said Jacob. "Like a pitbull."

"Huh?"

"You sank your teeth into the crazy situation around here and aren't letting go until the truth has been uncovered. Are you always like that?"

Natalie squirmed uncomfortably. "Sure. My parents are journalists—it comes naturally, I guess. Can we go into your dad's office for a minute? I want a closer look at the stack of papers in his cabinet."

Jacob pulled out his keys. "The newspaper articles?"

"Yeah."

Suzy looked curious, but didn't demand an immediate explanation. They entered the caretaker's room and looked around.

"Cool. I've never been in here," said Suzy, reaching into a box of brightly colored chalk and taking out a handful. "Your dad's got everything."

"And apparently, he keeps track of it all religiously," said Natalie.

Suzy dropped the chalk back into the box.

Jacob grimaced. "Used to. He and his computer are both down for the count right now."

Natalie walked over to the cabinet and pulled open the door. "Did you find anything on the computer's hard drive?"

"Couldn't get it working. I'll give it another shot tonight," said Jacob. "Thank god the database is located on that server downtown."

Natalie carried a stack of articles over to the bare desk. "I keep flashing back to that broken machine. It's like the attacker was trying to annihilate it. Get rid of evidence or something. Anyway, can you guys help me go through this stuff?" She went back to the cabinet and took out the rest of the clippings.

"What are we looking for?" asked Jacob, picking up a short article in a community paper about Eddie being named MVP.

"Not sure. Just tell me if you come across anything we don't already know."

Natalie started scanning the pages. Isaac had squirreled away any press that mentioned Western over the past two decades. Some of the articles were crumbling with age. Next to her, Jacob and Suzy peeped up every once in a while to read something aloud, but didn't come up with anything Natalie hadn't been able to find out on the Internet or by talking to people.

She was about to give up when Suzy came across a short profile of Eddie Chango that ran in a local weekly magazine. There was a fierce photo of him squinting into the sun, holding a football clasped to his chest. The reporter praised him as one of the best players in the city, and asked how he maintained his school obligations at the same time as practicing five days a week. He responded that he wasn't going to be class valedictorian but he'd maintained a C average. While playing football, he was surprised that his grades had actually gone up quite a bit.

"When was that written?" asked Natalie.

"Last February," said Suzy.

"Football season ends in early December," said Jacob conversationally. "They pick next year's senior players in the spring."

"I read something dated around the same time, an interview with a couple guys who also mentioned their grades," said Natalie. She shuffled through the pile and picked up a *Star* article on jocks who juggle school and team pressures, passing it to the others. "Here. I remember the piece because Mark Wallin and Jamie McCallum are in my math class. I recognize them from the photo. They joke about their grades improving dramatically: 'Overall, our teammates do better at school when they're playing.'"

"That *is* odd," agreed Jacob, skimming it. "You'd think the amount of time they spend at practice and working out would mean the opposite."

Suzy looked blank for a moment, then clued in. "You're saying in an oh so cryptic way that someone might have doctored their grades?"

"What are the chances several guys' grades would spontaneously improve because they're getting more exercise?"

"Zero to nothing?" suggested Suzy.

"That's my guess," confirmed Natalie. "I think we've seen everything we need to here. Can I borrow this article about Mark and Jamie?"

Jacob shrugged. "Sure, I guess. Doubt my dad will even notice."

Natalie tucked it into her notebook. They put the rest of

the papers away and Jacob handed her back the tricked-out cell phone before they split up to go home. Natalie made it there just after five, almost an hour before her father was due. She spread out her geography and English homework on the kitchen table and made like a busy beaver.

Jorge beamed when he came in and saw her working. He started cooking and didn't seem at all suspicious about her extracurricular activities. It helped that he was preoccupied about having to leave extra early the next day to cover a press conference, then had meetings right through the evening.

The house was empty as she got ready for school in the morning. Why couldn't that have been the case last week, when she was skipping gym? Sandy didn't show her face in class again, so soccer was fun, but Natalie started to wonder what was up with the girl. Did their little "talk" upset her so much that she was actually hiding at home?

Geography class was on the dull side, as usual. At lunch, Ruth and Suzy chattered away to each other. Natalie wasn't much company. She was a girl obsessed. Her mind kept returning to Sandy, and to the superintendent's reaction when she told him about Eddie's complaint.

She dragged her feet to math, unsure how to handle things if Wojcik kicked her out again, and dreading being humiliated in front of a full class. He hadn't recorded yesterday's absence or there would have been a phone call home. Guess he didn't want anyone to know he'd thrown her out.

She sat down at her desk and kept a wary eye on the door. Wojcik hadn't arrived yet. Two minutes late, a harried-looking man with tight brown curls rushed in, apologizing: a substitute

teacher, who told them that Wojcik was off sick. Maybe he and Sandy were at home, having some kind of family conference.

As soon as school ended, Natalie sprinted to the office, determined to talk to Principal Jefferson. She entered and saw that the principal's door was closed. The receptionist was removing a stack of paper from a printer tray. She tucked it into a folder, which she put in an overflowing tray marked for the vice-principal. When Natalie plopped into a chair, the receptionist looked up.

"Can I help you?" asked the woman, leaning on a counter that separated her work area from the waiting area.

"I need to talk to Principal Jefferson. It's urgent."

The woman's voice was frosty when she spoke again. "Ms. Jefferson is busy at the moment. Would you like to leave a message?"

"I'll wait," said Natalie curtly.

"Suit yourself. But you'll have to tell me your name, so I can let her know you're out here."

"Natalie Fuentes."

It was obvious the secretary didn't approve of students barging in and demanding to talk to the principal. Or was it Natalie in particular she didn't approve of? Man, was she ever getting paranoid.

Jefferson's door opened eventually. Her "How can I help you?" managed to sound an awful lot like "What have you done now?"

"Can I speak to you alone?" asked Natalie, glancing at the secretary.

"Certainly. Follow me."

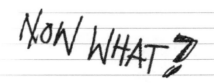

They went into Jefferson's office and sat down across the desk from each other.

"It's about Eddie Chango," said Natalie, jumping the gun.

It took Jefferson a moment. She must have been expecting Natalie to bring up Sandy again. "How do you know Eddie?"

"He's a friend of a friend. He told me he asked for an investigation to be made into his expulsion but never heard back from you."

"What are you talking about?"

Natalie tried again. "He tried to lodge a complaint when he realized Mr. Wojcik wasn't reporting the incident correctly. Yesterday, when I asked Mr. Winthrop about..."

Jefferson's confusion quickly morphed into annoyance. "Ms. Fuentes, first off, Eddie never lodged a complaint. I'd be the first to know about it, unless... unless I didn't get the message. I don't tend to reopen disciplinary actions after the superintendent decides on them. And my secretary is usually, um, overly competent."

"He did tell me he spoke to your secretary several times. Ask him yourself. It's his right, you know. I went to the board of ed's website. It's all up there. If there's reasonable doubt that the process was thoroughly investigated, a student or his family can ask for an appeal."

Jefferson sat back, contemplating what Natalie was saying.

"He would have filed an appeal, if he'd known what his rights were."

The principal stood up and went over to the filing cabinet, unlocked it and flipped through the folders to find Eddie's. She froze. "It's not here!"

"What?"

"Eddie's file!"

Natalie, of course, wasn't the least bit shocked. She'd figured all along that was the reason someone broke in. "Ms. Jefferson, regardless of what's in that file, there's a whole football team of guys missing their star player and two of them saw what happened between Eddie and Mr. Wojcik that day. If somebody bothered to ask, I'd bet they'd describe a situation a lot closer to Eddie's side of the story."

Jefferson sat back down and hunched in on herself, hands laced in front of her on the desk. "But Mike's report clearly detailed the event... That would mean he deliberately..."

"Lied?" finished Natalie, when Jefferson trailed off.

Jefferson's head snapped up. "What are you inferring?"

"I have a hunch that if you start with taking a closer look at Eddie's case, some of the other problems around here might resolve themselves. Superintendent Winthrop already agreed to reexamine the file."

Jefferson leaned forward to rest her chin on her hands. "And why, Natalie, would you think..."

Natalie decided it was time to go before she revealed anything that might get people she liked in trouble. She glanced at a clock on the wall and stood up. "Oh, look at the time. I've got to get home."

The bike nook was still deserted when she got out there. She was disappointed because she'd been hoping to find Ramiro and his buddies. Her father would be at work until at least ten, so she had the evening ahead of her and wouldn't have to make up excuses. The first thing she did when she got home was

email Ramiro, telling him to round up Eddie and meet her at school at eight. Her subject line was: "Urgent!"

Next she sent a message to Jacob, asking him to work his wonders and prioritize looking for clues on his dad's old hard drive. She wanted to know what it had been used for just before Isaac surprised the attacker.

She left the inbox open and went downstairs to throw a bowl of stew into the microwave. When it was hot, she went back upstairs. Jacob still hadn't responded, but Ramiro had, to say he and Eddie would be there. She changed into some long pants and grabbed a proper flashlight, rather than her dinky penlight, and the special cell phone.

A month ago, if one of her Brooklyn friends had suggested sneaking into high school late at night or on the weekend, she would've died laughing. She wasn't exactly an academic superstar, yet she'd already done so once and was about to do it again. She was glad to see Eddie's car pulled up on the sidewalk in front of the bike nook, though she frowned when she noticed the passenger seat door was open and the bass-heavy stereo was blasting. Not exactly inconspicuous.

Ramiro and Eddie lounged on the side of the car, eating pizza from a party-sized box. Ramiro pushed himself up with his elbows as she wheeled up. "So, Maggie, what's up?"

"I need to talk to Eddie."

"Well, you found me," said Eddie. Ramiro's face tightened. Natalie devoted a moment's thought to whether he was concerned, jealous or annoyed. She settled on concerned.

"It's you, isn't it?" she said, leaning her bike against a tree.

"Sorry?"

"You're the 'gremlin.' The one who's been borrowing school property."

His eyes flashed a warning. "What're you talking about?"

"I know it's you, Eddie. Don't play stupid. The stickers—I saw some on the back seat of your car when you gave me a lift home—the spray-paint, the so-called thefts..."

Ramiro's eyes widened but he didn't say a word.

"I didn't touch your locker."

"I know that. I'm referring to the blackened fruit, and other things."

When Eddie's mouth opened again, she didn't give him a chance to deny her claims. "Look, I don't blame you after everything you've been through."

Eddie's expression slowly shifted from angry to guilty. "It's the only way I could get back at Jefferson."

"Well, I think I've figured out a way to get your file re-examined by the school superintendent. But it means you're going to have to behave like the model citizen until the process is finished. No vandalism, no thefts—is that clear?"

"Okay, I guess," said Eddie, cautiously. "Let's hear your plan."

"Wojcik will get what he deserves. I'll make sure of that. He got you expelled because you refused to toe the line and wouldn't let him treat you like dirt. In my opinion, he's not above attacking Isaac Kaufman if he thought the caretaker was getting in his way."

"What a scumbag," said Ramiro, punching a fist into his other palm.

"Leave Wojcik to me," she said. "First, we need to put back

all the stuff that's gone missing, so no one can hold the thefts against you."

Eddie shifted uncomfortably. "I don't know what you're talking about."

"Don't play dumb, Eddie. The sports equipment that's been disappearing ever since you were expelled. Come on. As soon as the shit hits the fan, Wojcik'll come looking for it. I know you're not selling it and you're too smart to stash it at your apartment. Where is it?"

Ramiro prodded his friend with an elbow. "Hey, man, Maggie's right. If the stuff mysteriously reappears, it's like no crime was ever committed."

"If she opens her big mouth, I could be charged with mischief," said Eddie. His chin jutted defensively as he peered at Natalie, as if he was trying to see inside her skull, desperate to figure out whether she could be trusted.

"We're the only ones who know for sure and I'm not going to tell," said Natalie. "I came to you first because I owe you one—a big one—for saving me from Sandy and her Barbie gang after the party on Friday."

Eddie threw up his arms. "Fine! I'm going to trust you, *maldita argentina*. I better not live to regret it."

"You won't," promised Natalie.

"Follow me." Eddie set out on foot at a brisk pace. He led them straight to the football field and around the grandstand to a small wooden door that was hidden under the benches. It looked as if it hadn't been opened in ten years. The wood was splintered and coming apart. He bent down and tugged. It creaked with old age as it opened.

Natalie and Ramiro got down on their hands and knees to take a look.

Ramiro let out a low whistle. "That's a lot of stuff."

Eddie looked embarrassed. "Four or five loads?"

Ramiro shook his head in disbelief. "Should have brought shopping carts."

"Might as well start with these goalposts," said Eddie, reaching in and dragging out a long metal pole. Ramiro took the second one. They started walking, posts swinging in the wind, while Natalie grabbed a couple of boxes of tennis balls and hurried to catch up.

"Where are we taking this?" asked Ramiro.

"The courtyard," said Natalie.

"Why there?"

"It's about as far as we can get from the caretakers' office. We really don't want to be seen."

They stayed away from the school walls to avoid being caught in the security floods that lit the path as they made their way to the courtyard, dumped the stuff behind a bush and went back for more. Eddie picked up four dusty bases—it must have been hard for the baseball team to play without those. Natalie tugged on something fabricky that ended up being an enormous volleyball net. Ramiro grabbed a bin of flags.

"Thank god Eddie's getting reformed," said Ramiro, laughing softly. "Or our school's athletes would be city-wide laughing stocks."

Natalie had to stifle a giggle. Even Eddie grinned reluctantly.

They kept their eyes out for any stray caretakers or teachers, but things went as smoothly as could be expected. It took four

more trips to empty out the horde. By the time they were done, the guys had roared off in their car and Natalie was back on her bike, she was physically exhausted. But as soon as she was alone, her brain snapped into full alert. Western's gremlin would no longer be an issue, but Isaac's attacker was still at large.

Hoodie Guy

Chapter thirteen

atalie made it home again around nine, an hour before her father was expected. She ran up to her room and checked her email to see whether Jacob had responded. There was a message.

With a little cyber handholding from some geek friends, he'd been able to access the information on Isaac's hard drive by plopping it into one of his other computers and trying a couple of tricks. There wasn't much on it, but the cache did reveal that it was last used to access the school's student grade database.

After learning what he could from the cache, Jacob asked his father whether the attacker had been near the desk. Isaac confirmed that's exactly where the man was standing when he surprised him and demanded to know what was going on.

Natalie paused in her reading. The man must have panicked and knocked Isaac out to buy enough time to smash the incriminating machine. But Jacob should have mentioned earlier that the computer could access secure systems like the grading program. He'd told her it was only hooked up to the school intranet and the supply-tracking database. That must be why he'd looked so guilty: it was only *supposed* to be connected to those systems. He'd likely altered the machine's security level so that it could connect to off-limits programs. Someone must have found out, and was using the terminal to change students' grades.

It was now or never, Natalie decided, knowing full well that if she wasn't here when her dad walked in the door, he might never trust her again. But what was the worst he could do? Ground her? That would be hard for him to enforce, given his erratic work schedule. She wasn't ready to give up for the day, so close to unraveling the whole twisted situation.

Was she insane to take on Isaac's attacker alone? She had no choice. She refused to drag anyone else down with her if the plan backfired.

She barely hesitated before looking up Wojcik's home address on the Internet. He lived just over ten minutes away, near the school. She ran out of the house, praying her father wouldn't come back early, and pedaled like a madwoman, fueled by nervousness.

Outside Wojcik's, she paused to stash her bike behind a reddening maple tree. The place looked like every other single-family home on the street, except that high bushes boxed in the front lawn and hid the first floor from view. On the second floor, two lights were on at opposite ends of the house.

Some part of her knew she'd regret her decision to walk up the dark driveway along the side of the house instead of knocking at the front door. Unfortunately, walking up to the door and saying, "Hey, Sandy, one of the girls at school gave me your address—I was worried when you didn't show up at gym class" wouldn't exactly ring true, considering Sandy was

probably staying away from school because of her interaction with Natalie the previous morning.

Her instincts for caution did make her pull out the rigged-up cell phone and autodial Jacob's computer, clip the little microphone onto her shirt collar, and tiptoe silently up the gravel. She was still half-heartedly trying to think of a plausible excuse for her sudden appearance.

A couple of windows sat low on the building. She peered inside, but it was much too dark to see anything. She got an impression of wide open space—maybe a rec room. Did people still have rec rooms these days? Jutting out from the back of the house was a wooden deck partially lit by the lights inside the kitchen. She scurried to the middle of the yard, crouching to hide behind the porch.

A curtain was shut over the sliding glass door that opened into the kitchen, but it was semi-transparent. Someone was sitting alone at the table. It looked like Sandy.

Natalie climbed the stairs, staying flat against the brick wall. She could see the girl clearly now, reading in the middle of the room. Creeping forward, she noticed the sliding door was open. The curtain flapped a little in the wind. She moved closer, screwed up the courage to call to Sandy, and leaned in.

"Sand—*uurrk*."

A sudden shove from behind turned her words into a grunt. She flew forward, arms flailing as she tried to regain her balance. A second push made her pitch head-first into the hard back of a chair.

Pain exploded in her brain. Blackness descended. She felt nothing.

When she came to, she had no idea how much time had passed. She was sprawled awkwardly across a loveseat, and her head was pounding. Sandy perched on the far armrest, hands clasped in her lap.

Natalie fought the urge to relax into sleep by picturing Isaac Kaufman, stretched out motionless in his hospital bed. It was bad to sleep if you had a concussion. Somehow, she knew that.

She focused on Sandy's hands, which were squeezed so tightly the knuckles were bone white. Tilting her splitting head, she peered up at the girl's face and tried to make eye contact. Sandy just sniffled and angled her body farther away. Excellent. Black mascara smudges on her cheeks betrayed the fact she'd been crying. The girl was a total waterworks.

With a start, Natalie realized Mike Wojcik was sitting on a stuffed armchair across the room, watching. If eyebrows could kill, his would be committing murder right about now. In a how evil can you get? contest, he was miles ahead of Sandy.

Wondering again how long she'd been unconscious, Natalie remembered the mic clipped to her shoulder, and glanced down surreptitiously. It was gone. She brushed her fingers over her pants pocket and discovered that the cell phone had disappeared too.

"W—what happened?" she asked, finally.

Wojcik smirked. "You were out cold. I didn't even have to hit you. One shove and your clumsiness did the job for me."

She lifted a hand to her forehead. Sure enough, her fingers came away sticky with blood. Her body ached for sleep. She closed her eyes, then forced them open again and shook her

head to wake herself up. Terrible idea. Splinters of pain pierced her skull.

"You look pathetic," said Wojcik.

"I—I'm bleeding."

"I can see that. You're not the same confident girl who was trying to break into my house half an hour ago, are you?"

Thirty minutes. Jacob should have listened to the recording by now. Had she given him enough information to figure out where she was? She licked her lips, hoping her mouth would start to work properly. "W-wasn't breaking in. I just needed to talk to Sandy."

Wojcik shook his head and sighed. "Don't lie, Natalie. I don't like girls who lie."

She wished she could think of a good retort. All that came out was, "Wh—what?"

"You know the old saying: 'You're either with me or against me'? It's clear which side you're on," he said calmly.

"Unlike the jocks whose grades you've been illegally improving?" Natalie asked. She'd finally managed to formulate a full sentence without stuttering!

Wojcik's face was blank. He didn't even acknowledge her accusation about the grades.

"He's talking about Eddie Chango," chimed in Sandy, speaking for the first time. "I told him all the freak boys from Western are falling over themselves to protect you."

Wojcik's eyebrows raged at Sandy now. She squeaked pitifully.

"Stop intimidating her," said Natalie, wondering why she was helping her own tormentor.

"In case you're wondering, we found your cell phone," he said, pointing at a small mass of electronic parts smashed against the wall. Was it still recording? Highly unlikely.

"Who were you talking to?" he demanded.

"Sorry?"

"It was on."

"No, it wasn't."

"You're still doing it. Lying." He leaned forward in his seat to rest his elbows on his knees. "Was it Eddie? Or one of your other good-for-nothing friends? Ruth Hamilton? Jacob Kaufman?"

When she didn't answer, Wojcik shot across the room and grabbed her by the chin. He twisted her face upward, so her neck was angled awkwardly. She tried to pull away, but he just squeezed harder, pinching her jaw. A slow, mean smile twisted his lips. From this angle, he looked every bit as threatening as the attacker in Isaac's office.

"It really doesn't matter," he said. "I've already called the cops and told them everything. They're on their way to arrest my little intruder."

A sob burst out from Sandy. Why was she crying? She wasn't the one who was about to be arrested!

Wojcik was momentarily distracted by his niece's emotional distress. He let go of Natalie and gripped Sandy's shoulder, shook her hard. "Pull yourself together."

Sandy's mouth opened and closed as she gulped air.

"You're completely useless," he continued. "You almost ruined everything by drawing attention..."

"The cops will never believe you," said Natalie, hoping to

Wojcik's eyebrows

transfer his focus back to her. "I know you were the one who attacked Isaac Kaufman. I bet the sneakers you were wearing are somewhere in this house."

He laughed and shook his head at Natalie, like she was a misbehaving child. "That's where you're wrong. It wasn't me. Besides, this is my house and you're an unwanted guest. I'm your teacher. Who are the cops going to listen to?"

Her heart sank. He was right. Darkness was seeping in between the venetian blinds covering the window on the far wall. Her father would be home by now and probably wondering where she was. What would he do when he got a phone call from the police?

"You're just like the rest of them," said Wojcik, out of the blue. "An immigrant loser whose parents barely speak English and can't afford to dress their kids properly. Western wasn't always this way. When Jefferson was hired, she opened the doors so wide you all came swarming in, taking places that should have gone to kids who deserve the privilege of attending a fine institution, and disrespecting those of us who worked so hard to make it that way."

"Eddie was the last straw for you?" she guessed, when he fell silent. She wished the phone was still recording, so that monologue would have been saved on Jacob's computer.

Wojcik snorted. "When things started to disappear, Eddie was playing right into my hands. I love that kid. He's so dumb, he doesn't even realize he's my ace in the hole."

"But Eddie never hit you!"

"Irrelevant. Jefferson was unable to cope with the vandalism. She's been this close to breaking for months." He pinched

his thumb and forefinger close together. "The attacks on Isaac proved that she doesn't have the balls to crucify a petty thief, and can't even fathom that one of her students might be a violent criminal. Don't think that fact escaped the school board superintendent's notice."

"You're the one who attacked Isaac Kaufman, not Eddie!"

"I told you that wasn't me. And if *I* were in charge, I'd have crushed Eddie like a bug."

Sandy stood up right then and took a couple of steps toward the door. Wojcik leaped across the room and positioned himself between the girl and the door. She cowered backward.

"Where do you think you're going?" he demanded.

"To do my homework," said Sandy.

"Oh, no, you're not. You're staying right here so you can tell the cops what happened." He nodded toward Natalie. "That nosy little bitch broke into our house."

"You're out of your mind!" yelled Natalie.

"I can't lie for you anymore," said Sandy quietly.

Lightning fast, Wojcik grabbed her by the ponytail and yanked her head back. Sandy's gasp of pain turned into a quivering lip. Considering the fact that Wojcik was Sandy's legal guardian and she really had nowhere else to go, she was in a rough situation.

Wojcik finally let go of her hair. Sandy hiccuped and quickly stepped out of arm's reach, head bowed. When she spoke, her voice was so soft, Natalie almost didn't hear the words. "I'm sorry."

"You'd better be," said her uncle.

Natalie's head jerked up, pretty sure Sandy had been talk-

ing to her, not him. She searched Sandy's face for some hint the girl might grow a spine. Wojcik walked away and flicked open the blinds impatiently. When he took a seat again, his body was facing the window. As the minutes ticked past and Sandy didn't so much as look at her, Natalie's confidence faltered.

The doorbell rang. Wojcik bobbed up and out of the room, pausing only to snap at his niece, "Make sure she doesn't move."

Sandy looked miserable. Her hair was coming out of its ponytail and her cheeks were splotchy red. Natalie sat forward, ignoring the blast of pain in her head, and whispered, "Sandy, it's the cops. You have to back me up. Don't let **him drag** you down anymore. He's a monster."

Natalie's words pushed Sandy back over **the edge**. She started blubbering like there was no tomorrow.

Out in the hall, Wojcik was greeting some men.

"Natalie Fuentes, did you say?" boomed a voice that Natalie recognized. Detective Lewis, just her luck.

"Sandy!" Natalie hissed, making the girl jump. "Pull yourself together. Even if you hate me, your uncle's about to get away with ruining both Principal Jefferson and Eddie's lives. You can stop him."

Sandy scrubbed her eyes with the back of one hand. The men's voices out in the hall were getting closer. Wojcik entered the room and gestured for the two detectives to follow him.

"We meet again, Ms. Fuentes," said Lewis. He didn't seem all that surprised, but his eyes bounced from the blood on her forehead to Sandy's disheveled appearance. His spiral-bound notepad was poised for note-taking. Under his scrutiny, Sandy cowered even more.

"So, what seems to be the trouble here?" he addressed Wojcik.

Wojcik lifted a finger to point at Natalie. "This young lady broke into my house. She must be the one who's stealing things from the school."

"I didn't break in!" protested Natalie. "I wasn't even in the house when he pushed me from behind. I just came to talk to Sandy—she's in my gym class. I know I should have gone up to the front door and knocked, but..."

"Liar!" shouted Wojcik. "Search her pockets and her bag." He kicked the canvas bag on the floor toward Lewis.

The detective looked annoyed at the command, but stooped to pick up the bag and empty the contents onto the loveseat next to Natalie. She gasped when a Palm Pilot, a cell phone, and an expensive-looking men's watch fell out.

"This is the watch I saw on Isaac Kaufman's attacker, I swear!"

Lewis was flipping through his notepad to find her description.

She scooped up the watch to look at the face—but it wasn't the same one. They could all see it had a blue Jets logo. She dropped it, flustered.

"Don't believe a thing she says! Empty your pockets, girl," snapped Wojcik.

Natalie did so. In one pocket she found a crumpled wad of bills—Canadian and American—and in the other a jumble of gold and silver jewelry that looked as if it might be Sandy's. She dropped everything on the loveseat cushion.

Wojcik pounced on the little pile. "My Palm Pilot!"

"I've never seen any of this stuff before in my life!" insisted Natalie.

Lewis put a hand on Wojcik's shoulder to restrain him. "Sir, you're tampering with a crime scene. We're going to take these items down to the station to be fingerprinted. If we identify Ms. Fuentes' prints on the items in her bag, we'll be able to prove beyond a doubt she's guilty."

"I don't care about any fingerprints," sputtered Wojcik. "This is my house. She broke in. Ask my niece."

All eyes aimed at Sandy. Wojcik grabbed her wrist and ground out from between clenched teeth, "Tell the detective exactly what happened, Sandy."

Sandy covered her face with her free hand and sobbed.

Lewis stepped forward. "Release her arm, sir."

Wojcik dropped the wrist as if it was burning him.

"Ms. Wojcik," said Lewis, in soothing tones. He put a big hand on her shoulder.

"It's Blatchford," she sobbed.

Lewis looked inquiringly at Wojcik.

"I'm her uncle and legal guardian."

"Ms. Blatchford, I understand you're upset," said Lewis slowly. "Can you nod or shake your head in answer to some questions?"

Sandy nodded, a single jerk of the head between wracking sobs.

"Did you catch Ms. Fuentes breaking into your house?"

Sandy shot a quick glance at her uncle. His jaw was clenching and unclenching spastically. She gave the tiniest of nods, then leaped up and ran out of the room.

Thanks a lot! fumed Natalie to herself.

"Natalie, I'm afraid I'll have to take you and your bag of loot down to the station for booking," said Lewis. "I have to say, I'm very disappointed in you."

"No!" she yelled. "Sandy feels guilty. Look at her. That's why she's crying her head off."

Lewis reached for Natalie's arm to help her up.

She jerked away. "Go talk to her alone. She's terrified. This is all a set-up. He hates Eddie Chango. He got him expelled from school on purpose..."

Lewis was studying her closely, trying to figure out how she knew so much about the situation, but at least he wasn't trying to arrest her at the moment. A definite improvement.

"I suppose you're going to say I've been committing acts of vandalism too," said Wojcik, as if he was talking to a very naughty girl who had been caught making up stories.

"I don't know about that," she said. "That's the one part of the mystery I couldn't solve." There was no way Natalie was going to drag Eddie into this.

"According to my police scanner, that situation's been resolved," said Lewis. "The night caretaker found the missing equipment outside the school two hours ago."

"Search his house," she pleaded. "You'll probably find Eddie's student file here somewhere."

"The detective doesn't have time to listen to your stories, Natalie," grated Wojcik.

At those words, Lewis decided it was time to look alive. "Save your breath, Ms. Fuentes. You're going to have to tell the entire story again down at the station."

This time, when he grabbed her arm, he held on firmly. Once she was standing, he twisted her wrists behind her back so he could snap on a pair of handcuffs. He led her out of the living room and into the hallway. Natalie stared up the stairs to the second floor. Sandy was hovering at the top, watching.

"Tell them the truth!" Natalie yelled. "Stop this, before anyone else gets hurt. Before he hurts *you* any more."

Sandy stepped backward, out of view.

Lewis's partner opened the front door and Lewis pushed her out impatiently. They walked down to the street, where the police car was parked. Lewis opened the back door—the one for criminals. He put his hand on her head to guide her into the seat, shut the door, and stepped away to have a word with his partner.

Just then, Wojcik's front door banged open and Sandy flew out in her socks. Wojcik chased after her, looking murderous.

What now? thought Natalie, staring out the partly open window. Would she be accused of yet another heinous crime?

Sandy moved so that Lewis's body was between her and her uncle. "She's right. He's lying. About everything."

"Excuse me?" said Lewis, clearly shocked.

"He did all those things, except the attacks," said Sandy. "Those were done by his football players. He's really not a nice man. I'm so scared living here. Please help me."

chapter fourteen

 ojcik let out a choked scream and lunged for Sandy. "You little *bimbo!*"

Lewis whipped out his billy club and neatly hit the man in the back of the knees, causing him to do a face plant into the grass. "Looks like you have some explaining to do."

When Wojcik started to push himself up, a poke in the back from Lewis's club made him fall flat again. He turned to the side and looked up. His face was an angry red. "Don't touch me or you're going down for assault!"

"Resorting to threats won't get you any place good," boomed Lewis, a warning in his voice. "I won't touch you unless you do something you shouldn't, like attack your niece. And you'll talk sooner or later. If not you, then one of your football players, who's offered a sweet deal to rat you out, certainly will. The truth always come out."

After that, Wojcik regressed to screaming threats at everyone within hearing range, but he looked so ridiculous lying there on his stomach, with Lewis hovering over him, that no one was too concerned about him following through on them.

Natalie slumped against the car seat in relief and listened to Sandy spew out incriminating information about her uncle.

It was as if a stopper had been removed from her mouth.

"He showed his favorite football players how to improve their grades on Mr. Kaufman's computer and then held it over their heads. Just before you got here, he planted all that stuff on Natalie so you would think she's guilty. He hates Eddie because he's racist. He hates Jefferson too. Plus, he wants her job. He's been trying to destroy them both."

No wonder it had felt like being body-checked when the intruder slammed into her, Natalie thought. A football player would hit hard. Wojcik had managed to tear the school apart without getting his own hands dirty.

"His football players attacked Isaac Kaufman both times because they thought he knew they were using the terminal," continued Sandy. "This last time, he actually interrupted one in the middle of changing his grades."

"He didn't know a thing," said Natalie, sighing. "He had no idea it was happening."

In the end, Lewis released Natalie and transferred the cuffs to Wojcik's wrists. The man wouldn't stop shouting, so Lewis shoved him in the back of the car and shut the door.

He asked Sandy if she had any friends she could spend the night with. When she ran inside to call Lynette, he pulled out a cell phone and asked for Natalie's phone number. He wanted her father to come pick her up. She did everything she could to convince him that wasn't a good idea, but he didn't budge. To her surprise, when Jorge came on the other end, instead of listing all the horrible things she'd done, the cop informed her father that Natalie had helped him solve a crime that had stumped the entire community for nearly a year.

Not that it made her dad any more lenient. The first thing he did when he arrived was inform her she was grounded for a month. He proceeded to lecture her the entire time they were collecting her things and putting her bike into the car's trunk. She distinctly saw Linebacker Lewis hide a grin behind one of his beefy paws. They drove off with Jorge loudly listing all the reasons she was in trouble. When they got home, he told her to go up to her room and stay there.

Flanked by the incredulous Hamiltons, she rode to school the following morning in a daze. The siblings started pumping Natalie for details as soon as she shut her front door. Apparently, Missy had called Matt after talking to Lynette and Sandy the night before. Natalie was out of breath by the time they were at the corner.

Matt filled her in on what happened after Detective Lewis booked Wojcik down at the station. He'd stopped by Lynette's to talk to her parents. Sandy asked if she could finish the year at Western, and Lynette's parents offered their guest room for as long as she needed.

Natalie was a hair's breath away from being late when she raced to the gymnasium. As she was reaching out to grip the gym doors, a page came over the P.A. for her to report to the office. She turned around and went to see Jefferson.

"You must be Natalie," said the secretary when she entered the room. The woman had already met her twice, but now she was grinning like the Cheshire Cat. "So lovely to meet you."

When Natalie raised a hand to knock on Jefferson's door, the secretary said, "No need to knock, honey. The door's always open."

"Thanks," said Natalie, a little flustered. What a different reception than last time! She twisted the doorknob and entered.

To say Jefferson looked haggard was an understatement. Her fitted shirt, a buttery blue leather number, looked as if it had been bunched at the bottom of her closet before she put it on this morning. But when she saw Natalie, her face lit up. "Have a seat, young lady."

Natalie perched on the chair.

A giant yawn threatened to dislocate Jefferson's jaw. When she was good and finished, she spoke. "Natalie, Detective Lewis has filled me in on your escapades."

Natalie nodded, thinking: Fight or flight?

Jefferson stifled another yawn. "Look, the truth is I should probably be disciplining you right now, but I'm just too tired. I have to line up a permanent replacement for Mike Wojcik and I was up all night, doing an inventory of all the equipment that suddenly reappeared on our doorstep. I assume you're responsible for its return..."

"I don't know what you're talking about," said Natalie, a little too quickly.

"Right," said Jefferson, doubtfully. "Well, I wanted to let you know I've called Eddie Chango and apologized for not responding to his calls."

"That's great," said Natalie, a grin spreading across her face.

"Not taking Eddie's calls was a bad oversight on my part—and my secretary's, of course. She was trying to lessen my workload, which I appreciate, but in this instance it led to a deserving young man being kept out of school. Superintendent Winthrop and I are reviewing the incident that led to his expulsion. You'll probably be seeing him in your classes as early as next week."

"I think he should get a public apology," interjected Natalie. "His reputation's really taken a hit because of all this. Everyone thinks he's a thug. But he's not. He saved me from getting beat up on Friday."

Jefferson's jaw dropped. "Beat up? On school property?"

"No. On a street near my house, after the dance."

"Oh. Well, something public isn't a bad idea," agreed Jefferson thoughtfully. "By the way, I'll be expelling the two football players—"

"Jamie McCallum and Mark Wallin?" guessed Natalie, flashing back to the newspaper article in Isaac's office about the jerks in her math class.

Jefferson nodded. "They're responsible for the actual attacks. And I'm still considering disciplinary action against Sandy Blatchford, so if there's anything I should know..."

"Sandy's suffered enough, having Mike Wojcik as her uncle."

"I suppose you're right about that," said Jefferson. "You've also probably saved Mr. Kaufman a great deal of future pain." Suddenly, she reached out a hand for Natalie to shake. "Young woman, Western owes you a big debt for untangling the secrets that have plagued this school. Thank you."

Natalie blushed. "It was nothing."

Jefferson raised an eyebrow to indicate she disagreed. "Just try to stay out of trouble from now on, all right?"

"I'll do my best," said Natalie.

"Why do I think that's not much of a promise?" asked Jefferson, pulling an admit slip out of her drawer and scribbling on it.

Natalie accepted the admit slip and left the office, smiling ruefully. Now that she had the golden ticket, she was in no rush to get back to gym. As she made her way downstairs to sit in the empty geography classroom, a second page went out over the P.A. calling Jamie and Mark down to see Jefferson. She took advantage of the free period to read ahead in her textbook and finish an assignment due today.

Jacob arrived with the first couple of students and chose a seat next to her. "You did it! I have it on the best authority that Wojcik's been fired. Turns out he was even hoarding keyboards and chalk brushes he'd stolen from Western's supply orders in his garage."

"That's what I heard too."

"'Bout time we got rid of him."

"Yep."

"So what are you doing for dinner?"

"Tonight? I've got to spend some time convincing my dad I'm not a total delinquent," she admitted. "I'm probably in for another lecture about personal safety and the importance of focusing on my school work. Secretly, he knows I'm a hopeless case."

"Hopeless?"

She shrugged. "There was this one time, while we were living in Texas for a few months, and my parents were investigating the story of a Native activist on death row, when I managed to stop a couple of kids who were stealing school

supplies from the smaller kids and selling them for a profit. Their parents were in the local motorcycle gang, so everyone was scared of them."

Ms. Rahman called for silence and began a lesson on the climate's impact on vegetation north of the tree line. Natalie discovered that everything up there was edible, that there were no poisonous plants in the arctic. Good to know. Toward the end of the period, the teacher stepped out of the room and the students were supposed to work in pairs on a series of exercises.

Jacob pulled his desk over to hers. "You're going to have to tell me all about your adventures some day. Besides, my dad will want to thank you for figuring out what was going on."

"Wow. News sure travels fast."

He winked. "My father got a call from Jefferson last night."

"Ahh. Give me a couple of evenings alone with my dad and things should get better at home. I'm supposedly grounded, but he'll probably have forgiven me by Friday..."

"Friday should be fine," said Jacob. "By the way, it's a good thing you were carrying my phone after all. Before Wojcik smashed it, enough of the conversation between him and Sandy was recorded to help incriminate him."

"Wow. I'm glad it wasn't sacrificed for nothing. Sorry about that. Can I buy you a new one?"

He dismissed her concern with a quick wave. "Small price to pay for keeping my dad safe."

At lunch, he came out to the courtyard with her to wait for Ruth and Suzy so they could head out for Wednesday grilled cheese. But when Missy and Lynette walked up, he took off, growling, "We'll talk later."

"Natalie!" Missy giggled, feigning surprise, and her laughter was like silver bells, very seductive. "I'm having a small gathering on Friday night—just a few select people. My parents are in Cancun for two weeks."

"Oh, yeah?" said Natalie, looking around for her friends.

An irritated look flickered across Missy's face at the lack of enthusiasm. She took a fuzzy pink diary out of her designer handbag and ripped out a sheet of paper, scribbled down her address. "Nine o'clock. Be there. Bring Ruth Hamilton if you want. Her brother will be coming." Her tone of voice made it clear Natalie and Ruth were only invited because of Matt.

Natalie unenthusiastically accepted the piece of paper. Just then Ruth bounced up. Her arms jerked forward and then fell flat against her sides. She'd been about to do a cartwheel when she noticed Missy standing there.

Missy nodded stiffly, linked her arm through Lynette's, and left without another word.

"What'd Miss Bitch want?" asked Suzy, eyes on the girl's departing back. She'd been right behind Ruth.

Natalie crumpled up the piece of paper in her hand. "To invite us to a party."

Suzy and Ruth looked at each other meaningfully.

"What's the look for?" asked Natalie, frowning.

"You do realize what just happened. You were invited to the Golden Girls' party," said Suzy. "It means you've been accepted."

"You're popular!" said Ruth. "From now on, you'll be going to all the best parties, and the hottest boys in the school will fall in love with you. I guess that's the end of us. She's not going to want to hang out with you and me, when she's being offered that!"

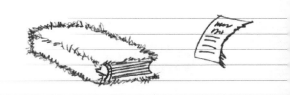

"The charmed life!" said Suzy.

"Next thing you know, Missy will be taking you to her country club," added Ruth.

"I already have plans for Friday night," said Natalie, shaking her head. "And, in order to join Missy's club, I'd probably have to dye my hair blonde and get blue contacts. No, thanks. I'd look terrible. Hunger's affecting your brains. Let's go eat."

She tossed the piece of paper with Missy's address on it into the nearest garbage can, put her arms around Suzy and Ruth, and steered them off school property.

She was dead on about her dad's grounding. It lasted three days. On Friday night, she walked up the Kaufmans' front path with butterflies in her stomach. It wasn't as if she hadn't been here before, seen Jacob's bedroom and met his dad. It just felt different this time, after everything that had happened. She was responsible for getting the man responsible for the attacks on Isaac thrown in jail.

When she rang the doorbell, Isaac answered, not his son. His expressive face bunched into an impish grin. He looked much better—his skin was a healthy color and he seemed stable on his feet.

"You look great," she said.

"I do, don't I?" He danced a little jig to demonstrate just how good he felt, but had to lean against the wall for support when he was done. "I'm not quite as good as new, or at least back to where I was before those bastards got their hands on me. But I'm getting there."

"That's a relief."

She followed him to the kitchen. He spoke over his shoulder as they went. "It must have been difficult for June Jefferson to believe just how bad things were in Mike's head." Isaac tapped his skull with an index finger to accentuate his point. "June's not a bad woman, she just likes her rules. Takes a lot to make her see past them."

They rounded the corner and entered the kitchen. Jacob was setting the table. Natalie gasped when she saw the feast. Having had macaroni and cheese last time she was here, she certainly didn't expect it. In the middle of the table sat an enormous platter heaped with grilled vegetables of all kinds surrounding a full salmon that had been broiled in fresh herbs. There was also a loaf of homemade egg bread, soup and potato pancakes. Unlit candles stood upright in a metal candelabra.

"This looks incredible," she said.

Isaac clapped his hands gleefully. He'd been watching for her reaction.

"Tell me about it," said Jacob. "I've been waiting to eat for two hours. I forgot to mention my dad's a great chef, didn't I?"

She narrowed her eyes in a mock glare. "I guess you did."

"Tonight, we celebrate the Sabbath, which starts at sundown," said Isaac, sitting down at the head of the table and reaching for a pack of matches. He said a brief prayer in Hebrew as he lit the candles. Next, he reached for the egg bread and ripped off a hunk, before passing it to Natalie. She looked at Jacob, unsure what to do.

"I thought you were Jewish!" said Isaac.

"Not really. I mean my mother is, but how did you find out?"

"A little thing called the Internet," said Jacob.

"According to Jewish law, if your mother is, then you are!" proclaimed Isaac.

"I guess, but she's secular."

"Ahh." Isaac sounded disappointed. "Well, it's never too late to learn tradition."

"Come on. What we do isn't very traditional at all," said Jacob.

"I suppose that's true," admitted Isaac. "But it's a ritual, and that's important."

He poured them all a glass of sweet red wine from a jug she hadn't noticed, and held up his glass for a toast. He suggested they go around and each say something they were grateful for that happened in the past week. "Me, I'm grateful for my health back."

Jacob thought for a moment before saying: "I'm grateful to have people I can trust in my life."

"I'm grateful for my new friends," said Natalie.

They clinked glasses and drank.

As they were eating, Jacob said, "I'm really just grateful you're getting better, Dad. I can't believe this all happened because Wojcik was scared you knew too much."

"A man like Mike Wojcik, he takes any opportunity to hate that he possibly can," said Isaac.

When dinner was over, Jacob and Natalie went upstairs. They'd offered to clean up, but Isaac shooed them away and started doing it himself.

"To be honest," said Natalie, once they were up in Jacob's room. "I'm glad you invited me to dinner."

"Why?"

"It gives me a chance to talk to you alone. I know what you did to your dad's computer: you changed the security level or something, and it could access things like the students' grades, not just your father's database."

His body went rigid. "Crap. I was hoping you wouldn't..."

"I'm not going to tell anyone what you did, if that's what you're worried about."

"You're not?"

"Hell, no. It's useful to have someone like you on my home team."

He let out a deep breath.

"I just don't want any secrets between us, or between me and your dad. Nothing that could become weird."

"It's just a bit of an adjustment letting you into my life," he admitted. "I don't have many friends. I've known Ramiro since I was about six. Eddie too. There are a couple other guys... mostly online. I'm a bit of a loner."

"That makes two of us," said Natalie.

"Really? You make friends so easily."

"You mean the Hamiltons and Suzy?"

"And you're confident around Ramiro and his friends."

"Confident, sure. Trusting, not so much. I guess I even make my zine because I'm some bizarre mixture of outgoing and shy."

"I like that about you."

"You do?"

"Definitely."

Natalie watched his face change into a shrewd grin.

"Now, about your website..." he said.

"What website?" she asked in confusion.

"Your zine needs a website. I've decided."

"You have?"

He nodded and opened up a browser window. "You're the biggest hacker chick I know."

"I am?"

"Yep. It's all about whether you can find alternate routes to solve a problem. Besides, you hardly make more of a distinction between private and public property than I do. You're a natural hacker. You just need to apply those same instincts to the Internet."

"Huh."

"I've already registered the URL www.nataliefuentes.com. I'll show you how to throw up a simple site you can update on your own later. You can sell copies online, post your archives and do whatever else you want."

"Wow."

He spent the next couple of hours teaching Natalie basic HTML and putting up a site with bare bones pages. At nine o'clock, she got up and stretched for the first time, amazed at the progress they'd made. "I've got to head home. My dad still has me on a short leash."

Jacob uncurled his thin body from his desk chair. "I'll ride with you."

"You don't have to do that," said Natalie.

"I know. But I want to."

"Well, I had a good time tonight. You're even stranger than me, and that's saying a lot."

"Thanks. I'd rather be strange than boring, any day."

She raised an eyebrow. "You don't have to worry about that."

They stopped on their way out to say goodbye to Isaac, who was working in the back room at a counter covered with molds of various kinds, tubs of white goo and enamel paints. Half-finished figurines were grouped together according to their scenarios. An unpainted gingerbread house sat behind miniature Hansel and Gretel, dropping bread crumbs as they walked up the front path. A scene from Shakespeare's *Hamlet* showed three witches stirring an enormous cauldron. Natalie could almost hear them chanting, "Double, double, toil and trouble. Fire burn, and cauldron bubble."

Thinking of her dad when he was down in the darkroom, Natalie was worried they'd be disturbing him. Quite the opposite; Isaac was thrilled to see them.

"Wait!" he commanded. "Before you leave, I want to serve you my homemade ruggelach."

"I can't stay any longer. My dad barely agreed to let me come over tonight."

"Then take some home for later. Jacob, go pack some cookies for her. I have to give her the present I made."

Jacob left the room.

"A present? That's really not necessary, Mr. Kaufman."

"Nonsense. You helped me very much." Without another word, he shuffled to the other side of the room and picked up a small handmade cardboard box. He turned back to her and handed it over. Natalie was dying to open it, but wasn't sure if it would be polite.

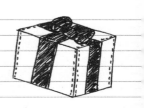

"Go ahead. Open it!" he commanded.

She carefully pried open the lid and lifted out a wad of tissue paper. Beneath it lay a tiny figurine that looked suspiciously like Nancy Drew, only she had dark hair streaked with fuchsia and was holding a silver magnifying glass the size of her head.

"I love it!" she said, tears prickling the back of her eyes. Impulsively, she leaned over and gave Isaac a peck on the cheek.

He grinned broadly, took the figurine from her and carefully replaced it in the box. She zipped it into her inner jacket pocket. It forced a funny square-shaped lump in the fabric just below her collarbone.

As Jacob and Natalie rode to her place, conversation came in spurts. He asked questions about her mom, the countries she'd lived in, her dad's job, and how she started making a zine. She answered him quickly, breathlessly, afraid to say anything that might give him a bad impression.

When they got to her house, Ruth was on the porch next door, leaning against the steps with headphones on. Natalie didn't notice any immediate reaction to seeing the two of them together. Her greatest fear was that Ruth would be angry.

Quite the contrary. By the time they pulled up into the driveway, Ruth was bouncing excitedly on the sidewalk. She didn't look angry at all. In fact, she ran over and hugged Natalie. "I just got a phone call from a reporter at the *Star*. You're some kind of celebrity."

"No, I'm not," Natalie started to protest as she swung her leg over the bicycle seat.

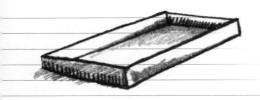

"Oh, don't be modest. You're incredible!"

Natalie glanced over at Jacob.

He was still sitting on his bike. "You are. If anything, I played Watson to your Sherlock."

"I never could have done it without all your homemade gear."

"Oh, listen to you two. Get a room!" groaned Ruth, sticking a finger in her mouth as if she was going to puke.

Natalie and Jacob both blushed. Ruth's eyes flitted back and forth between the two of them with a knowing expression. Natalie had no idea what to say.

Jacob recovered first. "I think I'll be going."

"See you later," said Natalie, as casually as she could.

He rode away.

"He's totally into you," said Ruth.

"You think so?"

"Don't play dumb."

"You're all right with that?"

Ruthie hugged her again, then pushed her forward down the front path. "Of course! He's so last week for me. Too skinny. I'm in love with someone else now."

Natalie's head snapped around. "Who?"

"Uh-uhn," said Ruth, shaking her head. "It's a secret. Let's just call him the tattooed man."

Natalie stopped in her tracks. "Not Eddie?"

"He's a tragic figure, don't you think? Kind of like Heathcliff from *Wuthering Heights*."

"You're not supposed to be reading those gothic romances, Ruth," said a voice at the Hamiltons' front door. Matt's lanky

frame leaned against the door. "Mom says you're too *impressionable*. I say you become incredibly annoying."

Just then, the front door of Natalie's house swung open and her dad's head popped out. "Nati? I thought I heard you out here. You were supposed to be home fifteen minutes ago. Come inside. Your mother's on the phone. She got your present this afternoon."

Natalie laughed at the timing and ran into the house before she could hear how Ruth responded to her brother's insult. There were so many new people and things in her life, that her first day at school felt like a million years ago. Her head spun just thinking about everything that had happened in the past two weeks.

She realized she had no clue what her life in Toronto held for her, or what kind of mystery would pop up next. But she was pretty sure of one thing—there was no way it would be boring.

about the author

Award-winning author Emily Pohl-Weary has been called "an unconventional and modern-day hero to many young female writers." Her first novel was described as "a candy kiss hiding barbed wire...as fun as eating a Ferrero Rocher."

Strange Times at Western High is her fifth book and her first for young adult readers. Emily's published works include a novel, a book of poetry, a biography of her grandmother, the sci-fi writer Judith Merril, and a series of comics. She was the recipient of a 2003 Hugo Award and a finalist for the Toronto Book Award.

One of her favorite childhood memories is reading the Nancy Drew mysteries over and over again. Emily's Natalie is a character any teen girl today could relate to.

Pohl-Weary edits and publishes the saucy hybrid lit/art mag *Kiss Machine*. Her cultural articles have appeared in numerous magazines. She lives in Toronto, Ontario.

Visit Emily Pohl-Weary's website at
www.emilypohlweary.com